THREE BY KATE GREY

BY HIS DESIRE
HIS ONE DESIRE
ONLY DESIRE

Kate Grey

By His Desire
Copyright © 2012 by Kate Grey

His One Desire
Copyright © 2012 by Kate Grey

Only Desire
Copyright © 2014 by Kate Grey

All rights reserved. No part of this publication may be reproduced, distributed or transmitted in any form or by any means, including photocopying, recording, or other electronic or mechanical methods, without the prior written permission of the publisher, except in the case of brief quotations embodied in critical reviews and certain other noncommercial uses permitted by copyright law.

This is a work of fiction. Names, characters, places, and incidents are a product of the author's imagination. Locales and public names are sometimes used for atmospheric purposes. Any resemblance to actual people, living or dead, or to businesses, companies, events, institutions, or locales is completely coincidental.

Book Layout ©2013 BookDesignTemplates.com

Three By Kate Grey/ Kate Grey. -- 1st ed.
ISBN 978-1-4953768-9-4

CONTENTS

BY HIS DESIRE
1

HIS ONE DESIRE
101

ONLY DESIRE
221

BY HIS DESIRE

CHAPTER 1

"Can I make a comment that will probably piss you off?"

Keith Logan glanced at his assistant, Valerie. "Nothing's ever stopped you before."

"Yeah, but I usually rip you about work-related stuff, and this is personal."

Keith turned back to the million dollar painting he'd just lent to the Modern Art Museum. "Go for it," he said, knowing she would anyway.

"I think you should start spending your money on something that will make you happy."

He frowned. "I am happy."

Valerie shook her head firmly. "No, you're not. And ever since you bought that painting it's even more obvious. You get this expression on your face whenever you look at it, like . . ." Her voice trailed off.

"Like what?" he asked in spite of himself.

"Like you want something you can't have. And that's not the look of a happy man."

Keith slid his hands into the pockets of his three thousand dollar suit. "I see. And your solution to this supposed problem is to throw money at it? That's not like you. You usually encourage me to throw my money at hospitals and homeless shelters."

"Yes, and I'm not going to stop doing that. But it wouldn't hurt for you to spend something on yourself." She gestured towards the painting, a portrait of a young woman. "I was actually glad when you bought this thing, because you wanted it so much and I thought it would make you happy. But it hasn't. So my advice is to spend a few weeks just . . . you know, indulging yourself. Go to Paris or London or some city you love. Spend obscene amounts of money for world-famous chefs to cook your favorite dishes. Pay high-class escorts to fulfill your wildest sexual fantasies."

He raised an eyebrow.

"Okay, so I was joking about the last part. But you could indulge in a few crazy one-night stands."

"What makes you think I'm not doing that already?"

Valerie rolled her eyes. "Oh, please. I've been your assistant for three years. I can tell when you're getting laid. The last time was . . ." She frowned, thinking. "Two months ago? No—two and a half. That advertising exec, what was her name? Horrible woman. I hated her guts."

This conversation was starting to bug him a little.

"Her name was Emily, and she wasn't horrible."

"She was cold as ice and totally ambitious. The worst possible match for you. I just thank God she dropped you for that idiot senator. But whatever. I don't really care what you do, as long as you do something. You've been coming to the museum every day to stare at that painting, and you're starting to look a little . . ." She hesitated.

"A little what?" he asked irritably.

"Grim. Dark. Foreboding. And frankly, it's getting old. I feel like I'm working for Heathcliff and Mr. Rochester and Edward Cullen all rolled up into one."

"Edward Cullen?"

"Pop culture reference. He's a vampire. He broods."

"So if I stop brooding, you'll leave me alone?"

Valerie sighed. "I just wish you'd figure out the one thing in the world that would make you absolutely, ecstatically happy—and go after it."

His gaze returned to the painting. "I'll take it under advisement. Now, if you wouldn't mind actually earning your salary, I'd appreciate it if you'd go to the auction we were discussing and bid on that first edition."

"Fine, fine. What are you going to do?"

"Figure out what would make me absolutely, ecstatically happy. Which may turn out to be firing you."

She grinned at him. "You wouldn't last a week without me. Later, boss."

He listened to the efficient clicking of Valerie's heels as she walked across the marble floor, leaving him alone in the big gallery. He actually would have a hard time functioning without her. She was efficient and irreverent and smart as a whip, and the fact that she was a lesbian was a bonus.

As an extremely well-heeled bachelor, he often had to deal with female employees who had decided he was the husband of their dreams. It was a relief to know there was at least one woman in his life without romantic designs on him. All he had to deal with from her was an annoying tendency to fuss over him like an overprotective sister.

As he stared at the portrait in front of him, he wondered what Valerie would say if he told her that once upon a time, he'd actually known what would make him absolutely, ecstatically happy.

Sarah Harper.

The portrait had been painted by her father, the famous artist, and he had captured his subject perfectly. Sarah had looked exactly like this in high school. Beautiful and intelligent, with a face like eager flame behind a veneer of shyness.

He'd never been able to break through that shyness. All his life, his money and good looks had been enough to charm everyone he met . . . except for Sarah. She was the only girl who'd ever haunted his dreams, and he'd never made a dent in her reserve. During the four years they'd gone to high school together he could hardly get her to talk to him, much less go out with him.

They'd graduated and gone on to different colleges, and for the most part Keith had forgotten about her. But every so often she'd pop into his head, always with a hot surge of remembered lust. Something about Sarah had just . . . done it for him, and even years later the memory of her could still affect him. So when Julian Harper passed away and a few of his unsold paintings showed up in art auction catalogues, Keith paid attention. His own father had died six years ago, leaving him an enormous fortune, and now, for the first time, he was actually glad he had nearly unlimited funds at his disposal. They enabled him to buy the portrait he was looking at right now.

Sarah was sitting on an overstuffed sofa with her feet tucked up under her. She was wearing a green dress exactly the color of her eyes, and her long mahogany hair was loose around her shoulders.

He wished he could have brought the painting home right away, but the auction house's arrangement with the Harper estate included a month-long showing at the museum before the purchaser could take possession. He still had one week to go before the portrait would be his.

"The museum will close in fifteen minutes," the p.a. system announced.

Keith checked his watch. Considering how much money he'd donated to this place over the years, the staff probably wouldn't kick him out at closing time if he wanted to stay. But he'd been here for more than an hour already. It was time to go home.

He turned to do just that, and froze.

Sarah Harper was standing in the middle of the gallery, looking right at him.

* * *

Sarah's body flushed hot, as though she'd stepped under a heat lamp. Keith Logan was standing just a few yards away. She recognized him immediately, even though it had been ten years since she last saw him.

Her first instinct was to run and hide, as if she were a little girl instead of a grown woman. Her eyes actually went to the exits, as if she were planning her getaway.

Then she took a deep breath. What was she thinking? She needed to pull herself together and go say hello.

And she would. Any second now.

Move, feet. Move.

If she'd been prepared to see him, she would have taken the time to put on emotional layers of protection—enough to cultivate a polite, relaxed demeanor and a friendly smile. But as it was, she felt awkward and exposed, as if she were back in high school again with a secret crush on the most unattainable guy on the planet.

Her palms were actually sweating.

Okay, enough. She managed to put some kind of smile on her face as she forced her legs to carry her forward.

"Keith. Wow. It's been a while, huh?"

His face was completely blank, which was a little disconcerting. "Sarah. Hi."

When he held out his hand she would have killed for the chance to wipe hers on her jeans before she took it.

But Keith didn't seem to notice that her palm was sweaty. His fingers tightened around hers in a warm grip, and a shock of awareness went through her. She wondered if he could sense how fast her heart was suddenly beating.

She pulled her hand away with a jerk, and then blushed. She was acting like an idiot in front of the man who had paid a million dollars for one of her father's paintings.

She looked up at the painting in question. If it had been left to her, she would never, ever have sold it. But the portrait, along with everything else, had gone to her stepmother.

"So I heard you, um, bought this," she said, wincing inwardly at the inanity of the statement.

When Keith didn't say anything, she glanced at him again. He was looking at her, not the painting, with a kind of focused intensity in his blue eyes.

She wondered if she had a foam mustache from the cappuccino she'd drunk earlier. The urge to brush a thumb over her upper lip was almost unbearable, but she remembered what her therapist had told her about that kind of self-consciousness.

It wasn't a reflection of reality. Let it go.

Maybe Keith was just comparing the way she looked now to the way she looked in the portrait.

"He, um, painted that the summer before I went to college. So of course I look older now."

His gaze didn't waver. "I was thinking you look exactly the same."

She did? Was that good or bad?

Keith, on the other hand, didn't look exactly the same.

He looked better.

Broad shoulders in a perfectly tailored suit. Black hair, blue eyes, chiseled features. And most of all, a sense of controlled masculine power that sent a tickling sensation to the corners of her body—the insides of her elbows and the soles of her feet and the hollows behind her knees.

Just like in high school, her intense awareness of Keith Logan made her blush like a furnace. She may have made huge strides in dealing with her social anxiety disorder in the last several years, but right now, at this moment, it felt like she was seventeen again.

Time to go, Sarah.

She opened her mouth to say a polite goodbye.

"Have dinner with me tonight."

She stared at him, her mouth still open. He'd spoken the words abruptly, without smiling, which made her wonder if he'd felt obligated to ask—because they'd known each other in high school, or because of the painting, or something.

"Oh . . . that's nice of you, Keith, but I . . ."

"Do you have plans?"

Still abrupt, and still no smile. His blue eyes narrowed a little as he studied her, and something about that focused gaze made her answer honestly. "No, I was just going home."

"To write?"

He knew she was a novelist? "Well . . . yes." She wrote historical fiction, and was currently working on a story set in ancient Ireland. "My editor is expecting the first draft next month, so I have to keep my nose to the grindstone."

"You need to eat, though. Right?"

This was starting to feel surreal. Keith Logan, one of the richest men in the city—not to mention the guy she'd had a crush on all through high school—was pushing her to have dinner with him.

"Um..."

"We'll go around the corner to Michael's." Then he held out his arm.

In a daze, she took it.

The feel of his strong, suit-covered bicep under her hand was so distracting that she stumbled on the edge of the carpet in the museum lobby. Immediately that powerful arm was even closer, around her waist.

"Okay?" he asked.

She looked up to tell him she was fine, but the words caught in her throat.

He was so close she saw the shadow of stubble on his jaw, and the scar on his left temple she remembered from high school. He was so close she caught the faint scent of really expensive cologne.

He was so close she felt the warmth of his body through his elegant suit.

"Yes," she finally managed to say. "I'm fine."

Except that she wasn't. She wasn't anywhere close to fine.

But it was just dinner. An hour, maybe an hour and a half.

She could get through one meal with this man, no matter how awkward and self-conscious she felt around him. It would be a kind of milestone. If she could deal with this, it meant she could deal with any social situation.

One dinner was nothing. One dinner, and then she'd never see Keith Logan again.

* * *

He couldn't let this be the last time he saw her.

And yet he knew by the time their entrees came that she wouldn't go out with him again. He'd asked, casually, what she was doing that weekend, and she'd said she was busy. No details—just that she was busy. When he'd asked more specifically if she wanted to get together for coffee sometime—because everyone had an hour for coffee, right?—she said no, thank you. Again, no explanation: just that polite no thank you.

Quick and clean. The perfect brush off.

He'd brushed off plenty of people in his life—including many, many women—but he'd never been on the receiving end. People didn't brush off billionaires. It just didn't happen.

He'd surprised her into having dinner with him, but she wasn't going to let him catch her off guard again. No, Sarah Harper had apparently decided that this was a one-off, never to be repeated.

It wasn't because she disliked him—or at least, he didn't think so. She seemed interested in their conversation when he stuck to neutral topics—books and music and art—and she even smiled a few times. She seemed a little tense and uncomfortable, but she'd always been like that, and not just around him. Sarah had always been shy.

Maybe that was it. Maybe she just felt shy. Maybe if he dropped the whole second date thing and just kept her talking, she'd loosen up enough to agree to go out with him.

Because he wanted to see her again. He wanted that with an intensity that pulsed through him like a heartbeat. He'd half hoped that going to dinner with her would be anticlimactic, that he would discover his attraction to Sarah had faded over time . . . but that's not what happened.

As he watched the gleam of candlelight in her brown hair and noticed how it set off the creamy translucence of her skin, his body reacted to her exactly the way it had in high school.

He wanted her.

Something happened to him when he was with her. Something primitive. His body hardened and tightened; his skin prickled with lust and adrenaline. On the surface he was still civilized, but it felt like he was hanging on to that veneer by a thread. Just below the surface, another part of him was howling like a wolf.

He wasn't sure why Sarah brought this out in him. It wasn't like she made any kind of effort to drive men crazy. She was wearing a pair of jeans and a gray cotton shirt—neat and clean and comfortable-looking, but not flashy or seductive in any way.

And yet he couldn't take his eyes off her.

There was a pause in their conversation as the waiter brought their dessert, and he took the opportunity to ask about something that had been puzzling him.

"If you don't mind my asking, why did you let that particular painting go to auction? You didn't feel a sentimental attachment to it?"

Her face flooded with color. "It wasn't up to me. All my father's unsold work went to my stepmother when he died."

Keith frowned. "He didn't leave you anything at all?"

Sarah avoided his eyes as she ran a fingertip around the rim of her water glass. "My father always believed that kids should have to struggle—especially if they want a career in the arts. Once I graduated from college, I was on my own. I understood that. I was fine with it. It was part of my father's philosophy."

"Bullshit."

That startled her enough that she actually met his eyes again. "What?"

"Sorry. But it is bullshit. Leaving you that portrait wouldn't have made a difference to you financially. You wouldn't have sold it, would you?"

"Of course not." Her voice trembled a little, and then, suddenly, words burst out of her in a torrent. "I love that painting. My father wasn't the kind of man who could express his feelings verbally, but he put his heart and soul into his work and . . . and when I look at that portrait, I feel connected to him. Of course I wouldn't have sold it. The truth is, I expected him to leave it to me. It never occurred to me that he wouldn't. I thought he knew how I felt about it. But . . . he was starting to forget things, these last few years. I was worried he was developing Alzheimer's but Lexie—my stepmother—said he was fine and refused to let me take him to a doctor. Maybe when he made his will he just . . . forgot."

Forgot his own daughter? You weren't supposed to speak ill of the dead, but if the guy could forget a girl like Sarah, he was an idiot.

"What about your stepmother? She could have given it to you, couldn't she?"

Sarah took a bite of her caramel custard before answering. "Lexie and I aren't exactly close. I did ask her about the painting once, but . . ." She shrugged. "Anyway, what's done is done. In the grand scheme of things, I suppose it doesn't matter. It's just an object, right?"

Keith didn't answer her. A crazy idea had come into his head. An insane, impossible, lunatic idea.

He took a deep breath and let it out slowly. He remembered all those things Valerie had said—that he should go after whatever would make him happy. That he should pay obscene amounts of money just to indulge himself.

It had never occurred to him to actually follow her advice. But why shouldn't he, just once, use his wealth to get the one thing in the world he really wanted? Would it be so bad to indulge this one forbidden fantasy—the fantasy that for all the years of his adolescence had found its way into every single jerk-off session?

The fantasy that Sarah Harper was in his bed. At his mercy. That he could spend hours . . . even days . . . doing things to her until he broke through her defenses and she gave into him completely.

It was crazy. And it would never happen. But if he had even one shot in a million, he was going to take it.

It wasn't like he had anything to lose. She'd already made it clear she didn't want to see him again. So what if she shot him down and left in disgust? The end result would be the same. If he was never going to see her again, did it really matter if she spent the rest of her life thinking of him as some guy she'd gone to high school with, or some guy who was so desperate for her he'd tried to bribe her into his bed?

He'd only had one glass of wine with dinner, but suddenly he felt drunk.

Shit. Was he really going to do this?

Sarah finished the last bite of her custard, and used her tongue to catch a drop of caramel sauce at the corner of her mouth. A strand of hair fell over her cheek and she lifted a hand to brush it back.

And then all he could think about was Sarah in his bed with that long brown hair spread out on his pillow.

What would it take to make her gasp? To make her moan?

To make her beg . . .

Fuck, yes, he was going to do this.

* * *

What had possessed her to say all that to Keith? He didn't care about her screwed up family relationships. He was always so cool and contained and perfect, and she wasn't.

He'd been that way in high school, too. She'd blushed and stammered her way through four years of hell while he'd sailed along effortlessly, smart enough to get good grades, rich and handsome enough to get any girl he wanted, and polite enough to treat even outcasts like her with kindness. He'd always gone out of his way to be nice to her, even when his friends rolled their eyes and made snide comments.

She had a sudden memory of their English class senior year. She'd sat in the desk behind his, and she'd spent the semester staring at the back of his head, at his black hair and broad shoulders and powerful back, and the way his arm muscles bunched and released as he read or wrote or raised his hand. He'd dated a few different girls that year, and Sarah had hated every one of them with a wholly unjustified ferocity. She had no reason to hate those girls except that they had Keith Logan's strong hands all over their bodies.

What would it be like to see behind that cool perfection? To be the one who could make those icy blue eyes turn hot with lust?

It was so hard to picture that Sarah wondered if, even in bed, Keith Logan stayed cool. That was easier to imagine. She could visualize him making a girl lose control while he stayed in charge.

She sighed as she finished her dessert. Dinner hadn't been too bad, all things considered, but it would be a relief to say goodnight. Being with Keith made her too anxious, and she hated reliving the feeling that had defined her adolescence: longing for something she could never have.

"Sarah."

She glanced up at him, admiring the way the candlelight drew out a gleam in his blue eyes. In this light they looked almost navy.

"Yes?"

"What if I told you there was a way you could have that painting?"

For a moment she just stared at him. What could he possibly . . .

Oh, no.

"If you're thinking about giving it to me, just forget it. There's no way, and I mean none, that I would let you do that. I didn't tell you all that stuff about my family to make you feel sorry for me, if that's what you're thinking."

She sounded almost fierce when she made that little speech, and Keith raised his eyebrows.

"I wasn't thinking that. And I'm not planning on giving you the portrait. Far from it."

She frowned. "I can't afford to pay you a million, and selling it to me for what I *could* afford—maybe ten thousand, if I'm lucky—would be the same as giving it to me for free. I'm not your charity case, Keith."

He was smiling at her now. "I hardly ever got to see this side of you in high school," he said.

She refused to be charmed by the famous Keith Logan smile. "What side?" she asked gruffly.

"This side. I remember you jumped all over Mark Sullivan once, because he said it didn't matter if public schools had arts and music programs."

He remembered that?

"He was implying that kids from working class families wouldn't appreciate 'the finer things in life'."

"Mark was an asshole."

"Yes, he was. But I don't think *you're* an asshole. I just don't want you to think I—"

"I am an asshole."

She stared at him. "What?"

"I am. Whatever good opinion you might have about me, I'm about to destroy it."

"What are you talking about? How?"

"With the offer I'm about to make you."

"What offer?"

He leaned across the table. "The museum has the portrait for one more week. When the week is up, I'll have the painting delivered to you. I'll transfer ownership to you legally. It will be yours."

"I told you, Keith, I—"

"Don't you want to hear my price before you reject it?"

She sat back in her chair and folded her arms. "Fine."

"In exchange, for one week, you'll live with me in my house. During the day, you can do whatever you want. There's a gym, an indoor pool, a library, a home theater. There's a study where you can write, and my chef will cook you anything you want to eat. But at night . . ."

He paused for a moment. "At night, you have to do whatever *I* want."

For a minute, it just didn't compute. She sat frozen in place, staring at him, while her mind flailed around helplessly trying to process what she'd just heard.

Keith's face wasn't helping. He looked like he always did—cool, calm, collected. His eyes were maybe a little more intense than usual, and as she stared at him, she caught the twitch of a muscle at the corner of his jaw.

After what seemed like a long, long time, she was able to force out a question.

"Are you serious?"

"Yes."

It still didn't compute. Was it possible that what he'd meant and what she was thinking weren't the same? As humiliating as it would be to ask, she had to know for sure.

Her heart was thudding against her chest. "When you say *whatever you want*—do you mean—are you referring to—do you mean sexually?"

Oh, God. Had she really just asked that? Was this conversation really happening, or was she lying in a hospital bed hooked up to a morphine drip, recovering from a car accident or a fall down the stairs?

One corner of his mouth lifted slightly. "Yes."

She couldn't sustain her current heartbeat and live. Her pulse was roaring in her ears, and she seemed to be staring at Keith through a kind of mist. Her whole body was buzzing and vibrating, like an engine being pushed too far.

She grabbed for her water glass and spilled some on the table. "Shit."

That corner of his mouth rose a little higher. "I think that's the first time I've ever heard you swear."

She took a quick gulp of water and set the glass back down. It still seemed impossible that he was serious about this, but . . . what if he was?

What if he was?

And then she had a realization as astonishing as the offer.

She wanted to accept. And not because of the painting. She wanted to accept because she'd wanted Keith Logan from the moment she'd laid eyes on him, back in freshman year at Adamson Academy.

But a man who was offering a million dollar painting in exchange for her sexual favors would surely expect more than she could ever provide. He would expect moves. He would expect tricks. He would expect *something.*

And then suddenly she was talking. She was talking in a rush about things she never, ever talked about. She was staring down at the white table cloth and the spot where she'd spilled the water, telling Keith Logan about her sexual history.

Such as it was.

"Look. Before you get any ideas about me, you need to know something. I've had two boyfriends in my entire life, and I only slept with one of them. And it sucked. Okay? It totally sucked. It hurt and I didn't know what I was doing and it *sucked*. For both of us. So we broke up, and I decided that the whole sex thing just isn't for me. I have, so to speak, a solo gig as far as all that's concerned. It's just me and my trusty vibrator. Do you understand what I'm saying here? I don't have the first clue what I'm doing in bed. I'm not exciting, I'm not adventurous, and I have no skills. I'm not the kind of woman you want for this . . . arrangement of yours."

She paused to take a breath, her stomach clenching in agonized embarrassment at the truths that had just spilled out of her.

"I don't want skills."

Her gaze jerked up to meet his. "Then what *do* you want?"

A wicked gleam came into his eyes. "I want you in my bed and at my mercy. And I want to ruin you for your vibrator."

His voice was low and raspy and the sexiest thing she'd ever heard.

This couldn't be happening. It couldn't.

There had to be something wrong with this scenario. What if he was into really freaky stuff? Stuff she could never, ever deal with?

She cleared her throat and stared down at her empty dessert plate. "What if you did something I didn't like? I mean . . . would I have to stay no matter what?"

He didn't answer her right away, and after a minute she looked up again. He was staring at her with a blank expression on his face. "Sarah. Are you actually considering saying yes?"

What did *that* mean? Was this whole thing a joke after all?

"Oh, God. You weren't serious, were you? Of course not. What an idiot I am. What a total—"

"*Sarah.*" One of her hands was fisted on the table, and now he reached out and covered it with his.

Sensation shot up her arm and through her whole body. His hand was warm and big and strong, and little pulses of pleasure emanated from where they touched.

"I've never been more serious about anything in my life. So let me answer your question." He leaned towards her again. "If something happens that you don't like, all you have to do is say so. You can call off the deal anytime. To get the painting, you have to stay with me the whole week, and you can't say no to anything. If you do say no, or if you want to leave, the only consequence is that you don't get the painting. That's it."

His hand was still on hers, and she found herself lost in his blue eyes. How many times in high school—and long afterwards—had she fantasized about being in Keith Logan's bed?

Her skin prickled with heat and desire.

He thought the only reason she would ever agree to this was because of the painting. But the painting had nothing at all to do with what she said next.

"Okay."

For a second he just stared at her. Then his hand tightened on hers.

"You mean that?"

"Yes. I'll do it."

Saying the words filled her with a kind of recklessness she'd never experienced before. She felt wild, like she might be capable of anything.

When the wave of recklessness was followed by a wave of anxiety, she reminded herself that she could call off the deal anytime.

The waiter came to their table with the check, and Keith let go of her hand. He took care of the bill, and then he met her eyes again. "I'll send a car for you tomorrow afternoon. What's your address?"

As she gave it to him in a shaky voice, she wondered what in the hell had gotten into her—and how long it would take to wear off.

CHAPTER 2

Keith had no idea how he got through the next day. He was useless for all practical purposes, and when Valerie finally asked what was wrong he just shook his head.

"Would you believe I'm actually taking your advice?"

"Yeah? It's about time. What advice, specifically?"

"It's a long story. I'll see you tomorrow at the board meeting."

He'd forced himself not to call his housekeeper about Sarah until now, when he was finally heading home for the night. He'd told himself that by not asking, he was at least giving himself one day to hope and anticipate, even if she decided not to go through with it after all.

But now, as he slid behind the wheel of his Jaguar, he pulled out his cell phone and dialed home.

"Yes, Mr. Logan?"

"Hi, Nancy. I was just calling to find out if Miss Harper arrived this afternoon."

"Oh, yes, she's settled in nicely."

He was filled with a relief so intense he felt almost light-headed. "Good. Great. How did she spend her day?"

"Well, she put her things in the guest room you'd told me to prepare for her, and I brought her a plate of cheese and crackers and a glass of Burgundy. She wandered around the house a little and spent a lot of time looking at your art collection in the upstairs gallery. Then she went into the downstairs study with her laptop and did some work. She had dinner about an hour ago."

"Did you give her my letter?"

"Yes. With the dessert, just like you asked. She went to her room after dinner, and I heard her filling the bathtub a few minutes ago."

His mind filled with the image of Sarah taking a bath in his house, and he almost drove off the road.

"Okay. That's good. I don't think we'll need anything else tonight, Nancy. Why don't you head home?"

"All right, Mr. Logan. Do you want Paul to stay?" Paul was her husband, and also his chef.

"No. I had a late lunch and I'm not really hungry."

"We'll see you tomorrow morning, then."

So when he pulled into his garage and went inside the sprawling mansion, he knew that he and Sarah were alone in the house.

It was eight-fifteen. He'd told her in his letter that he would come to her at nine o'clock, so he couldn't cheat and go now, even though his heart was pounding and she was all he could think about. But he was the one making the rules, and he wasn't going to break them.

So he went to his bedroom suite instead, loosening his tie as he climbed the stairs and pulling his clothes off as soon as he was in the room. Then he turned on his Jacuzzi shower and let the hot water beat down on his naked skin. He resisted the urge to jerk off for the hundredth time that day, even though he was starting to think he probably should, just to take the edge off.

Because he was so hard right now his cock could crush diamonds. He hoped Sarah had followed orders and put on the blindfold he'd left for her, because he was afraid the sight of his lust-crazed expression and raging hard-on might make her rethink their agreement, given how inexperienced she was.

And he was afraid that despite his promise, if she told him she wanted to leave, he wouldn't be able to let her go.

* * *

Sarah tried not to think about nine o'clock. Every time she did, a wave of anxiety made her stomach tighten and she wanted to run back home.

She didn't know what gave her the courage to stay. Maybe it was Keith's letter, which had been oddly reassuring.

At nine o'clock precisely, be on your bed in the blindfold you'll find under your pillow. You can wear whatever you want. And remember that you can't do anything wrong, because I'm in charge.

Had he guessed about her ever-present fear of doing something wrong? Or was her neurosis just really obvious?

Sarah took her time in the bath, shaving her legs carefully and trying not to think about Keith touching them later. Even with his reassurance, if she thought too much about what might happen tonight she knew she'd chicken out.

By the time it was ten minutes to nine she was so nervous her hands shook as she got dressed. She agonized over the decision of what to wear, and finally chose her favorite pajamas over the more risqué set she'd bought that morning at a boutique downtown.

She'd always secretly thought that she looked sexy in these, even if she'd had them for years. Something about the cut of the white cotton camisole top made her small breasts look firm and shapely and perfect. The bottoms were thin and soft from many washings, and felt wonderful against her silky smooth, just-shaved legs.

Underneath she wore the white satin panties she'd bought that morning. They were simple and elegant and made her butt look amazing, which she supposed was some justification for spending thirty dollars on underwear.

Five minutes to go. Something told her Keith would be punctual. She sat down on the four-poster bed, brushing her fingertips over the burgundy silk comforter. The blindfold she'd found under the pillow was silk, too—a simple black band she'd tried on earlier.

Three minutes to go. She looked around at the beautiful room—the antique furniture, the Aubusson carpet, the fireplace and the artwork on the walls and the floor to ceiling windows hung with burgundy velvet drapes.

One minute to go. She lay down in the center of the bed, resting her head on the pillow and sliding the blindfold over her eyes. Her heart was beating so hard she could hear it.

And then she heard the door open.

Her hands fisted involuntarily, and she found herself clutching the comforter. For a minute there was silence, and then she heard footsteps coming towards her.

A wave of goose bumps prickled her skin. She felt the bed give as a large male body sat down on the edge, and every muscle in her body tightened.

She heard a match striking, and there was a faint whiff of sulfur. Then she caught the sweeter scent of wax, and realized that Keith had lit the white candle on her bedside table.

"Candlelight becomes you."

His voice was low and raspy, like last night when he'd said he wanted her in his bed.

Was she supposed to say something in answer? A spasm of anxiety tightened her stomach muscles. She had no idea what the rules were, what he expected of her, what she was supposed to—

And then she remembered his letter.

You can't do anything wrong, because I'm in charge.

If he wanted her to speak, he could say so, or ask her a question. But since he hadn't done either of those things, she could do what she wanted.

And she wanted to stay silent. She wanted to take in everything that was happening, the sound of his voice and the scent of the candle and even her own nervousness. She had no idea what was going to happen next, but it was up to Keith and not her.

All she could do was wait.

"You mentioned last night that you like sweet wine, so I brought a bottle of that Hungarian Tokay I told you about."

He slid an arm behind her shoulders and helped her to sit up.

"Try this," he said softly, and then she felt the rim of a glass touch her mouth. She parted her lips, and Keith tilted the glass very slowly until she could take a sip.

It was like drinking light—so sweet and sinful she felt half-drunk from just a taste. She parted her lips again, hoping for more, and Keith gave a low chuckle as he tilted the glass again.

She took a bigger sip this time, relishing the way the wine bloomed on her tongue as it slid down her throat.

Then the glass was gone and something else took its place.

Keith's mouth was on hers.

It wasn't a kiss as much as a whisper of satin. The brush of his lips left hers tingling, and when he did it again she actually leaned into it.

The arm around her shoulders tightened, and his other hand slid into her hair. The pressure of his mouth was firmer now, and when she felt his tongue trace the seam of her lips she parted them eagerly.

And then he took her mouth for his own. His tongue was everywhere, stroking her until she felt it between her legs. Her heartbeat was thundering in her ears. The sensations were so overwhelming that she pulled back with a gasp.

Then she panicked. She'd pulled away. Was that allowed? No—it couldn't be. He'd said she had to do everything he wanted.

"Sarah."

His arm slipped from behind her shoulders and he settled his hand on her hip. She tensed up, waiting to hear what he would say next.

"There may be times this week when you say no or pull away but don't really want to end our deal. So when you say no or pull away, I'm going to ignore it. You might like the way that feels. But we'll need a way for you to tell me if you really *do* want to end our deal. So if you're serious about wanting me to stop whatever I'm doing, then I want you to say . . ." He hesitated a moment. "Abstract Expressionism. If you say that, then I'll stop, and we'll be done. Okay?"

He'd given her a way to freak out without ruining everything. She relaxed in relief, and nodded. "Okay."

"So let's try this out," he whispered, leaning close.

One of his big hands brushed up her arm, over her shoulder, into her hair. His thumb stroked the sensitive skin of her earlobe, and when she shivered in pleasure he did it again.

Then his other hand was on her left shoulder, and he slid one finger under her camisole strap.

A rush of sensation and anxiety made her stomach clench, and she felt herself stiffen.

"Tell me no," he said, and she realized that she wanted to. Not because she wanted him to stop, but because this was so new and intense she needed an outlet for her nerves.

"No," she whispered, and then Keith put his hands at the hem of her camisole and pulled it off so quickly she squeaked.

She covered herself instinctively, crossing her arms over her chest. Keith gripped her shoulders in his powerful hands and exerted steady, inexorable pressure to ease her down onto the bed. He grasped one of her wrists and pulled it up over her head, slipping something soft around it. He did the same thing to her other wrist. And then she was lying with her arms stretched over her head, her hands caught in velvet cuffs and her upper body naked.

Her heart thumped in her chest and her breath came in ragged pants. "Stop," she gasped, as Keith's mouth descended onto her breast. And then—"Stop," she said again, even as her back arched involuntarily to bring her closer to him.

His hand replaced his mouth, kneading firmly. "You can beg all you like, Sarah. I have no intention of stopping. Not until I've taken what I want."

Now both his hands were on her breasts, and it felt so good she squirmed, unable to stay still. She jerked against the handcuffs, and when she felt how securely they held her a flood of warmth surged through her.

His hands tightened until it almost hurt . . . almost but not quite. She wondered suddenly what it would feel like to cross that line, to move from pleasure to pain.

As soon as the thought crossed her mind she was ashamed of it. She didn't crave pain. She didn't want to be tied down like this. This wasn't her. This wasn't anything like—

And then the almost-painful grip was gone, and his tongue was there, drowning her in sensation as shockingly soft as his hands had been hard.

Oh, God. He sucked her nipple into his mouth, and she wished the rest of her could follow—that she could pour herself into him somehow. She did the closest thing she could and arched her back, and then Keith's hands slid under her shoulder blades and he held her suspended above the bed, swirling his tongue around her other nipple before biting down without warning.

It wasn't a hard bite but the shock went straight down her body, stabbing through her stomach and between her legs. Then he was soothing her with his tongue again, licking her softly and thoroughly. His hands slid out from under her, letting her settle down on the bed as he took her nipples between his fingers and thumbs.

He rolled the hard peaks back and forth with gentle pressure, and she felt it everywhere. He'd done something to her body—opened up a channel of sensation from her nipples to her—

Then he pinched her, hard, and the pleasure was so intense she cried out.

"Did you say something?" he asked softly.

"Stop, you have to stop," she said, even as the words turned into a moan.

Instead he pinched her again, not releasing her this time but holding her nipples tight even as he pressed a soft kiss against her throat.

He trailed his lips up her neck to her jaw line, and back down to her collarbones. On the way he touched his tongue to her skin in silken whispers.

And all the while he held her nipples in a hard, rough grip.

She was breathing in short little gasps, and she'd begun to twist underneath Keith's hands. She was feeling too much—too much pleasure and pain and everything in between, and in her core an aching blaze of want.

Keith withdrew his hands and his mouth, and Sarah's body quivered from the sudden loss.

And then he trailed one finger over the heart of her. "Your skin is so soft. Are you soft here, too?"

Oh, God. Would he be able to tell how wet he'd made her?

He touched her again, tracing the folds of her body through her pajamas, and she jerked away in a mingled rush of desire and mortification.

In the next instant he was holding her down, his hands like iron on her hips.

"You can't hide from me," he said in a low voice, and then he was tugging her pajamas and panties down her legs.

Goose bumps covered her bare legs and she actually fought against him, twisting onto her side and bending her knees against her chest. "Don't," she panted. "Please, don't."

"I'm going to see every inch of you."

He grabbed her lower legs, and then she felt the touch of velvet as he slipped the same cuffs around her ankles that he had used on her wrists.

Her legs were forced wide open, spread eagled in a V that exposed everything. Everything. All she could think was *my pussy, my pussy, my pussy* . . . a word she used in her internal monologues about sex, when she fantasized in her own bed at night—but had never used in conversation and tried not even to think when she was around other people.

But now it was all she could think about, because it was . . . *there*. On display. And as she lay still with no idea of where Keith was, since he wasn't touching her at the moment, she could only imagine that he was looking at her.

Looking at her pussy.

And as she imagined that, she became so painfully aware of how wet she was that hot color flooded her cheeks.

He still wasn't touching her. How did she look to him? What was he thinking?

The women he was usually with probably did the whole Brazilian wax thing. She went for regular bikini waxes, not because she expected a man to be spending any time down there but because swimming was her exercise and she spent three days a week in a bathing suit, even in the winter. So she was neat and trimmed but not . . . exotic.

He still wasn't touching her. Oh God, oh God, oh God. She was so much less sophisticated than the women he was used to. She'd been around women like that all her life, even if she'd been too crippled by her social anxiety disorder to be one of those women herself, and she'd always felt rough and unfinished next to their polished perfection.

She felt that way now. Rough and unfinished and exposed—literally.

And then, finally, Keith said something.

"Why, Sarah. I'm shocked."

His voice was low and husky, and the sound shivered along her nerve endings.

"You kept saying no, and all that time you were wet for me."

He trailed his finger over her again, but this time there was nothing between his skin and hers.

And then the most mortifying thing of all happened. His touch felt so good that she opened for him. The folds of her body parted with a little rush of honeyed moisture, and Keith's hand went still.

"Fuck," he whispered.

Every inch of her skin seemed to burn. She tried to squirm away from him, but he gripped her hip with one hand and covered her pussy with the other. "I don't think so," he said with a low chuckle. His big palm pressed against her, and when she squirmed again he pressed harder. And then, suddenly, she found herself digging her heels into the bed so she could bring her body closer to that insistent warmth.

"That's what I thought," he said, and she felt his body settling between her legs. "I'm going to taste you now, Sarah."

She froze. "Keith—no." It was the first time she'd used his name tonight. "I've never done that. I don't want to do that."

He used his hands to frame her, his index fingers on either side of her mound and his thumbs stroking softly over her tender skin.

"I'm going to do whatever I want to you. For as long as I want."

His thumbs pressed into her flesh as he parted her, and then his tongue stroked her inner folds in a slow, erotic slide.

Her body jerked as though she'd been shocked.

"Stay still," he ordered her.

"I . . . I can't."

One of his hands slid underneath her, and her whole body tensed when she felt the tip of his finger at her anus.

"Which would you rather have? My finger in your ass or my tongue on your pussy?"

Shit. "Your tongue!" she gasped.

"Where?"

She swallowed. "On . . . on my pussy."

His finger brushed lightly over her anus. "If you fight me, I'll fuck you here—with my finger if you're lucky and my cock if you're not. So I'd suggest staying very still while I eat you out."

Her heart thumped in heavy beats against her ribs. Keith put his hands on the sensitive skin of her inner thighs and caressed her softly from hip to knee, over and over, until the seductive gentleness of his touch became almost hypnotic.

No matter what happened, she would stay still. She could handle anything if it meant not having Keith's finger—or any other part of him—in her ass.

"Good girl," he said softly, and then his hands gripped her hips and his tongue was on her again.

Her cuffed hands fisted as she took a long, shuddering breath.

She'd fantasized about oral sex, of course. She'd fantasized about a lot of things she didn't do in real life. But her imagination hadn't prepared her for this.

His tongue was so soft. Like wet velvet. He was in no hurry at all, just licking her slowly and thoroughly until a low buzz of pleasure sparked deep in her bones.

She'd never experienced anything so . . . decadent. But how could this be enjoyable for him? Wasn't he tired of it yet? The longer it went on the more helpless and turned on she felt, and the more she wanted . . . *more*.

"Please," she heard herself say.

Immediately he stopped. "Please, what?"

She shifted restlessly, pissed at herself for saying something out loud and making him stop. "Please keep going."

"Exactly like I was? Or do you need something different? Something . . ."

He pressed his thumb against her clit, and it was so exactly what her body craved that she moaned.

"Something here?" he finished.

"Yes, oh yes . . ." Her embarrassment had disappeared, along with her inhibitions, and she pushed her hips off the bed and into his touch.

"That's it," he said softly, and then he was on her again, fastening his mouth on her clit and tonguing her, sucking her, his sudden urgency like a match to tinder. The sensations built so fast that she cried out, her wrists and ankles straining against the handcuffs as her orgasm swept over her like a tidal wave.

Her whole body quivered as she came down from the most intense climax she'd ever experienced. Her heart thundered in her chest and she couldn't seem to catch her breath.

After a while she realized that Keith was kissing his way up her body, soft and slow. The sensation heightened the aftershocks rippling through her, and if she hadn't been chained up she might have floated right off the bed.

"Keith," she said, the word coming out like a sigh.

He kissed her on the mouth, quick and hard and possessive.

Her nerves were still tingling. What would happen now? She was in a frame of mind to submit to anything he asked of her.

The truth was, she was eager. Which was why his next words were such a bucket of cold water.

"I think that's enough for tonight," he said, and then he was undoing the cuffs at her wrists and ankles.

When her limbs were free he helped her to a sitting position. He slid an arm around her waist and kissed her again, softer this time. His upper body was bare but he was wearing bottoms—sweats or pajamas or something like that.

He hadn't even taken all his clothes off.

She felt disoriented and bewildered. "But . . . that can't be all. You didn't . . . I mean . . . nothing happened for you."

He chuckled. "I enjoyed myself thoroughly, Sarah. And I have you for a whole week. That means I can take my time."

He said that, but if he really wanted her he would have taken her. She'd been ready, willing, and chained up, for God's sake.

Her post-orgasmic bliss was fading, replaced by the much more familiar taste of anxiety.

"Keep the blindfold on until you hear the door close. Then you can take it off." He kissed her again, and she felt him get off the bed. "Have a good day tomorrow,

Sarah. You'll get another letter at dinner with your instructions. I'll see you at nine o'clock tomorrow night."

She heard his footsteps, and then the door closing.

After a minute she took the blindfold off and laid it down on the bed beside her. Then she stared at the closed door and tried not to feel bereft.

Why had he left like that?

The most obvious answer was also the most depressing. Because the simplest explanation was that he didn't want her. Not really. Not in that overpowering, I-must-have-you-or-I'll-die sort of way.

The way that she wanted him.

She threw herself back on the bed and stared up at the ceiling.

This was high school all over again. She wanted him, and he didn't want her. Only now that feeling was brutally heightened, because he'd brought her to such a state of ecstasy before walking away.

She sighed and rubbed her face with her hands. Now that she'd come down from that unbelievable high, she felt tired. She should get some sleep, and maybe things would look different in the morning.

She started to reach for her pajamas, and then stopped. She wanted to sleep naked tonight. Keith might have confused her by leaving when he did, but her body still retained the imprint of his touch and she wanted to savor that.

The lights were off but the candle was still burning. Now she leaned over and blew it out, settling back into the darkness and the softness of her bed, pulling the blankets up to her chin and cocooning herself into them.

The silk sheets felt wonderful against her bare skin.

CHAPTER 3

A gentle knock at the door woke her.
"Miss Harper?"

Sarah blinked and sat up, remembering when the blankets dropped to her waist that she was naked. She pulled everything up to her chin again.

"Yes?" she called out, uncertainly.

The door opened and the housekeeper she'd met yesterday stuck her head in the room. "It's just me," she said with a smile. "I wanted to find out if you need anything, and if you're ready for breakfast."

Sarah glanced around the room, but didn't see a clock. "What time is it?"

"Nine-thirty."

"It is? Wow. I never sleep that late. Um . . . breakfast. Yes. That sounds great."

"Would you like me to bring you a tray, or—"

"Oh, no, I'll come down," Sarah said quickly. She didn't want Nancy to think she was some kind of lady of leisure who had breakfast in bed every morning. "I'll, um, be down in half an hour."

"I'll let Paul know."

Paul was the chef, she remembered. "Okay. Great."

After Nancy closed the door again she got out of bed and headed for the bathroom.

* * *

It should have been a perfect day. Breakfast was delicious—crepes with lingonberries, sausage sautéed with mushrooms, and the best latte she'd ever tasted, with Paul pouring espresso and hot milk from two separate containers into her cup, so they flowed together in one perfectly foamy stream. After breakfast she brought her laptop down to the library she'd fallen in love with yesterday, settling down at the antique desk between two bays of leather-scented books and preparing to work hard for the next several hours.

Only she couldn't.

When she realized she'd been staring at her screen for ten minutes, she got up and started to pace.

The library was ideally suited to pacing. It was big and empty and quiet, and with the enormous oriental rug on the floor her footsteps didn't make any noise.

She never had trouble concentrating on her work. From the time she was a child, concentrating on books or writing had been her escape from the pressures of social situations. So why couldn't she focus now?

Because Keith had invited her into his home so he could have his way with her, and then he hadn't. He'd pleasured her to the point of levitation without taking his own pleasure.

And suddenly, out of nowhere, she was angry.

Was she so undesirable? Or was he deliberately trying to torture her? Was this just a game to him, some kind of—

Well, of course it was a game. He was a billionaire indulging a whim. Some kind of weird whim of arousing her sexually without getting aroused himself.

Suddenly she laughed. She imagined telling someone about her dire situation. "So this gorgeous billionaire I had a crush on in high school offered me a deal. He'll give me the one painting of my father's I've always wanted if I stay in his mansion for a week being totally pampered, with plenty of time and space to work on my book—as long as, at night, I let him go down on me and give me the most intense orgasms of my life without having to do anything for him in return."

She wondered how many women in the world would trade their problems for hers.

It sounded perfect. It sounded like something out of a fantasy.

But it wasn't *her* fantasy.

In her fantasy about Keith, the one she'd had since she was fourteen, there was some kind of connection between them. They told each other things they didn't tell other people. They understood each other in ways no one else did.

It was a lonely girl's fantasy. A fantasy as much about the need for human contact as it was about a teenager's crush.

Sarah stopped pacing. She found herself in front of a deep leather armchair, and she sank down into it with her feet tucked under her.

She had friends now—good friends. People she'd met in college, or through her writing. She still struggled with social anxiety but she'd fought through it to the point where she was capable of making real friendships.

She didn't need to visualize Keith in that role anymore. But that wasn't the only thing she'd imagined about him, in her bed at night with the lights off. She'd also lusted after him. She still did. So how did she see him, sexually speaking?

She leaned back into the butter soft leather as she replayed the events of last night.

Beneath the layers of nervousness and embarrassment, she'd been turned on.

Really, really turned on.

Be honest with yourself, her therapist liked to say. *Life's too short not to know your own heart.*

She closed her eyes and let her mind sift through her sexual fantasies, past and present. The truth was, she'd always imagined Keith taking charge like he had last night. So it seemed that her idea of him had some root in reality. Maybe she'd always known that side of him was there, and some equivalent part of her responded to it.

So why did she feel so unsatisfied now? He'd taken charge, hadn't he? He'd blindfolded her and chained her up, for God's sake.

While he hadn't even gotten naked.

That night at dinner, she'd imagined Keith staying cool while he made a woman lose control. And that's exactly what had happened.

Another rush of anger swept through her. Why should Keith get to stay safe while she was so vulnerable?

Well . . . maybe because he was the one who'd set this whole thing up. He was the one who made the rules. He assumed that what she wanted was the painting, and in exchange, what happened between them at night would be on his terms.

Suddenly restless, Sarah pushed herself up from the chair and started to pace again.

She didn't have to stay. She could go. She could pack up and leave right now. That was the control he'd given her—the ability to end their arrangement at any time.

The one thing she couldn't do was try to change the rules, or control anything that happened between them at night. So she couldn't demand that he have sex with her or anything like that.

The absurdity of that notion made her laugh out loud. Imagine the girl with social anxiety disorder saying to the billionaire, "I insist that you fuck me immediately."

No. That would never happen. Even if she could find the metaphorical balls to say such a thing—which was, in itself, impossible—it would violate the agreement between them. She could do whatever she wanted during the day, as long as she did whatever he wanted at night.

At night.

She glanced at the windows, hung with drapes to protect the rare books from direct sunlight. But the sunlight was out there. It was daytime.

Nighttime was off-limits—and, by extension, whatever happened between them sexually. But that didn't mean she couldn't call him right now. She wouldn't talk about their bargain or anything sexual. But she could reach out to him.

* * *

Maybe he should just take the week off. Tell his assistant he was unavailable for board meetings and conference calls and business lunches.

Because as long as Sarah Harper was under his roof, he was going to be useless. Completely fucking useless.

She was all he could think about.

Last night, after he'd left her, he'd gone to his suite and straight into the bathroom, where he'd stripped off his pajama bottoms and stepped into the shower to jerk off. Later in bed he'd jerked off again, but he still couldn't get to sleep. He wanted Sarah so much it felt like his blood was on fire. He wanted to go back to her room and fuck her senseless.

Why the hell hadn't he when he had the chance?

She'd been lying there waiting for him, chained and naked and flushed with the orgasm he'd given her. She was every wet dream he'd ever had. She was *the* wet dream, the one girl he'd never been able to have, tied down and at his mercy the way he'd imagined so many times. He could drive himself into her and purge all that frustrated lust, all that hopeless longing. Wanting something you couldn't have made you weak, and now he had the opportunity to take what he'd always wanted.

To take Sarah.

So why hadn't he?

Going down on her had been intense. Maybe too intense. He'd never been so turned on by turning a woman on, even though he loved to make a woman come and always had.

But this had been different.

Maybe that's why he'd left. Because this felt different, and he wanted to be sure he had a handle on what was going on before he got in any deeper.

He wanted to be sure he had a handle on himself.

He was in his office downtown, where he was supposed to be meeting the chairman of one of his boards in half an hour. He scrubbed his face with his hands as if he could get Sarah out of his head that way.

Because he had to get her out. He had to stop thinking about her. He had to compartmentalize this, to relegate her to the place she belonged, to—

His cell phone rang, and when he glanced at it he saw his home number on the screen. A sudden chill ran down his spine. Nancy was the only one who ever used that number. Was she calling to tell him that Sarah was gone?

"Yes? What is it?" he asked brusquely.

"Did you ever have a pet?"

It was Sarah's voice. So she was still there, at his house.

Relief made him sag back in his chair. "What?"

"I was wondering if you ever had a pet. During high school."

"A pet?"

"Yes. A dog, a cat, a bird, a fish. A pet."

It was so damn good to hear her voice. But what the hell was she talking about? "I . . . what?"

"I was wondering, because back in high school the headmaster had that dog, do you remember? I think it was a Jack Russell terrier. And whenever you saw it you'd go down on one knee and let him jump all over you and lick your face, even if you were dressed up. So I wondered if you ever had a pet of your own. Because you don't now. Or if you do, you keep it in some part of the house I haven't seen yet."

He blinked. "You're calling to ask if I ever had a pet?"

"Yes." Her voice sounded almost belligerent, as though she might be mad at him. Was this because of last night? Had she not enjoyed herself? It had seemed at the time like she really, really enjoyed herself, but maybe something else was going on.

"Are you upset with me for some reason?" he asked cautiously.

"No. Why? Do I need to be upset with you before I can ask a personal question?"

Definitely belligerent.

"Of course not. I'm just surprised to hear from you, that's all. And the question's a little . . ." He hesitated. The fact was, he didn't particularly want to talk about pets or the lack of them. Because it *was* a personal question. And talking to Sarah about personal things was not going to help him with his problem—this feeling that he was getting in too deep.

"Now's not a good time for me."

"Okay. When should I call back?"

He got up from his desk and walked over to the window. "Sarah."

"What?"

"I don't think we need to talk like this. Do you?"

"I don't know if we *need* to or not. I just know that I want to. If you don't, of course that's okay. But if that's the case then I'll be heading home today."

Panic swept through him, and he gripped the phone as if it was a part of Sarah's body. "If you leave now you won't get the painting."

"I know."

Panic was followed by anger. "Jesus, Sarah. Why does it matter if I had a pet growing up?"

"If you don't want to talk about that, I'll ask something else."

"Like what?"

"Who's your favorite artist?"

He closed his eyes briefly. Okay, fine. If this is what it would take to keep her with him, he could put up with it.

He took a deep breath. "Edward Hopper."

"Really?"

"Yes. Why do you sound so surprised?"

"I don't know. You have so many impressionists in your collection, and a lot of medieval art, too. I guess I expected your favorite artist to be more . . . traditional. Classic."

"Edward Hopper is classic."

"I guess you're right. A modern classic. So why do you like him so much?"

"I don't know. I just always have."

"What's your favorite painting by him?"

"*Nighthawks,*" he said, glancing up at the reproduction framed on his wall.

"I love that painting. Why is it your favorite?"

He was starting to feel uncomfortable. Off-balance. If they hadn't started a sexual relationship last night, he wouldn't feel this way. It wasn't like he hadn't had conversations like this before. It was a first date sort of conversation, and God knows he'd had plenty of those in his lifetime.

But this wasn't a first date. Sarah hadn't wanted to go on a first date with him, which was why he'd bribed her into their current arrangement. And because it would only last a week, after which he didn't expect to see her again, he'd figured he might as well indulge himself completely. Give into urges he didn't usually express.

Most of the women he dated weren't into what he was, or else they were a lot more hard-core. He hardly ever found the right balance with a bed partner.

He wasn't into the BDSM scene. He'd visited a club once, and realized immediately that there was nothing there for him. He liked to dominate in bed but he wasn't into pain—not that much pain, anyway—and what he saw at the club felt staged and artificial.

He didn't meet many women he clicked with sexually, so his dominant side didn't come out too often. And on the rare occasions he did click with a woman that way, there had never been any other connection. They'd been short, hot affairs that ended amicably enough, and that was it.

Without realizing it, over the years, he'd put sex and relationships into two different boxes in his mind. Now Sarah was muddying the waters.

Suddenly he felt angry. She'd established her boundaries with him that night at dinner, and that was fine. But then he'd established his boundaries for her, and she was ignoring them.

And threatening to leave.

"I have a meeting in a few minutes. Have we talked enough?" he asked brusquely, without answering her last question.

"Enough for what?"

"Enough to satisfy you. Enough that you'll still be there tonight."

There was a short silence, which gave him plenty of time to realize exactly how much he cared about the answer.

"Yes, I'll be here."

"Fine. You'll get your instructions at dinner."

He ended the call, and then immediately regretted his abruptness. There was nothing stopping Sarah from changing her mind.

And no guarantee she'd be there when he got home.

His assistant buzzed him to let him know that his two o'clock appointment had arrived. He took the meeting even though he felt tense and angry, hoping he'd be less knotted up by the end of it.

He wasn't.

Once he was alone in his office again he started to pace back and forth. The more he paced, the angrier he got.

After a while he sat down at his desk, pulled out his stationary, and started to write.

He'd left a letter with Nancy that morning, to be given to Sarah at dinner like the night before. But now he had new instructions for her.

If they scared her off, so be it. But if she stayed, there'd be no holding back tonight. He'd take exactly what he wanted from her.

He called for a messenger to deliver the letter to Nancy and then did everything in his power to forget about Sarah for the rest of the afternoon.

* * *

He stayed in his suit this time, and he made her wait. He had a dinner meeting with some people from St.

Luke's hospital, where he was funding a new wing, and he didn't leave the restaurant until eight forty-five. It was nine-fifteen when he walked through the front door. Paul and Nancy had already gone home, so he and Sarah were alone—if she was still here.

He strode up the stairs without stopping at his suite, and stood outside her door for a minute. Then he set his jaw and pushed inside.

She was there. Relief flooded through him, followed by a wave of lust so intense it was almost painful.

She had followed his instructions, and was kneeling on the rug in front of the bed, naked and blindfolded. Her mahogany hair tumbled down her back, her lips were parted, and her hands rested on her bare thighs. As he closed the door behind him, he saw her hands fist briefly and then relax.

So she was nervous. Good. Then she knew what he'd been feeling for the last seven hours.

Adrenaline coursed through him as relief, desire, and anger coalesced into raw need. She looked so goddam sexy. Her nipples drove him crazy—small and pink and perfect. He remembered how they'd tasted last night, and the way his girl had shuddered when he bit and pinched them.

His girl? When had he started thinking of her as his girl?

She was here for exactly one week. She was most definitely not his girl.

He strode across the room until he stood right in front of her.

"Undo my belt and my zipper," he said, keeping his voice cool. He knew he was angry, and that a part of him wanted to punish her, but he didn't care.

If she decided to leave after tonight—or even during the night—there was nothing he could do to stop her. But if she decided to stay, she would damn well know who was the boss in the bedroom.

She reached up hesitantly and her hands met his thighs. He sucked in a breath as she groped her way towards his belt.

She found it. She explored the Italian leather for a moment and then undid the buckle slowly, her slender hands working precisely and carefully until she could slide it out completely and drop it on the floor.

Fuck. Something about the graceful efficiency of those small fingers made him hard as a rock. He felt off-balance, almost dizzy with desire. He opened his mouth to give another order, any order, with no purpose other than to assert his dominance—but then her fingers brushed over his erection as they settled on his fly.

All he could do was watch and try to stay upright as Sarah undid the button and lowered his zipper. She paused, and he knew that was his cue to tell her what to do next. But his mouth was dry and he couldn't utter a word. She hesitated, her face uncertain, but he still couldn't speak. A little frown gathered between her brows. Then her face cleared, and she gripped his pants and boxers in both hands and drew them down over his hips.

His erection sprang free and almost hit her in the face.

His hand shot out reflexively, and thank God one of the bedposts was within reach. He gripped it hard and somehow managed to keep from collapsing as Sarah touched him for the first time.

This was another point when he'd normally tell her exactly what to do, in a hard voice that made it clear who was in charge. But he didn't do that with Sarah. He was unbearably turned on by her tentative exploring and he couldn't bring himself to interrupt her.

It was obvious that while she'd probably done this a few times before, she wasn't experienced. There was a kind of shy curiosity on her face and in the way she touched him that he'd never encountered before.

Was it her inexperience that was so mesmerizing? Even as a teenager, he'd been with girls who knew what they were doing. He'd always thought that's what he preferred. So why was it so arousing to watch Sarah trail her fingers over his hard length, hesitantly at first and then with more confidence? Why did he have to grit his teeth to keep from groaning when she finally gripped him more firmly?

Then she touched her tongue to his head, tasting him, and it was a miracle he didn't snap the bedpost in two.

She was so cautious at first that he was caught between frustrated lust and a kind of fierce affection that was new to him. She was adorable. She was beautiful. And she was driving him insane.

She ran her tongue along his shaft, over and over, and then swirled it around his head before taking him into her hot, sweet mouth.

The sight of her lips wrapped around his cock short-circuited his brain. He'd fantasized about seeing her like this so many times, but he felt none of the triumph he'd always thought he would if he ever got Sarah naked and on her knees, with his dick in her mouth.

Instead he felt like he was standing at the edge of an abyss.

He needed to take control. He should tell her what to do, put his hand on the back of her neck to force her movements. *Harder. Faster. Deeper.*

But he couldn't. Her touch was so gentle, so hesitant . . . and yet it filled him with a pleasure so intense he vibrated with it. It was a strange, fragile ecstasy, and it scared the shit out of him.

And he couldn't do a thing but let it wash over him.

She was stroking the base of his cock with her hand while she took as much of him in her mouth as she could. Her long brown hair flowed down her back and over her right shoulder in a waterfall of silk, brushing over her right breast as she leaned forward. Her nipples were hard little peaks, and her whole body seemed flushed.

She was turned on. Christ, she was turned on.

He gripped the bedpost harder and tried to control himself. It was too much, too intense. He needed to end this. He should ram his cock into her mouth, forcing her to deep throat him.

But he couldn't do it. He couldn't do anything that might hurt or scare her.

Fuck.

Her movements were bolder now, and as she licked and sucked she suddenly made a little sound . . . an *mmmmm* of enjoyment that shot through him in a lance of pure heat.

His body tightened. He was going to come.

A strange panic seized him. He couldn't shoot in her mouth . . . not this first time. She wasn't ready for that.

He pulled away, but her hand still grasped him.

"I'm going to come," he said hoarsely. She leaned forward and put her mouth on him again, and it felt so good he closed his eyes.

When he tried to pull away again, she gripped the back of his thighs.

Shit. He'd let go of the bedpost, and when Sarah grabbed him he was thrown off balance. He went down on his backside as he caught his weight on his forearms.

Before he could recover his equilibrium she was between his legs, her hands on his hips as she licked and sucked him, her hair falling forward and brushing over his bare skin.

There was no stopping it. His body tensed with wild excitement before his orgasm slammed into him, and then he was shooting into Sarah's mouth as an explosion of ecstasy roared in his ears and melted his bones.

He groaned her name almost helplessly, again and again, as waves of pleasure pulsed through him. After what seemed like a long time he took a deep breath and let it out slowly, and became aware that Sarah was stroking her hands up under his shirt, which was still buttoned, and exploring the contours of his stomach and chest.

He was lying on his back with his weight braced on his elbows, and as he stared down at Sarah a spasm of terror squeezed his heart. She was naked and blindfolded and between his legs, having sucked him to near madness and brought him to one of the most intense orgasms of his life.

He felt undone.

She'd pushed his shirt halfway up his body in her exploring, but now she stopped and sat back on her heels.

"I want to take off the blindfold," she said almost shyly. "I want to see you." Then she reached up as though to suit action to words.

He jerked upright and seized her wrists in a grip so tight she cried out.

"No," he said, realizing how out of control this had unexpectedly gotten and how essential it was to reestablish boundaries.

"But Keith, I—"

"Don't say my name," he snapped. "You can address me as Sir."

He hardly ever demanded that his partners call him Sir. But when Sarah used his name another clutch of panic had made his heart tighten in his chest.

He couldn't stay, he realized suddenly. He needed to get the hell out of here and regroup.

And if she was still here tomorrow, things would have to be very different between them. He'd gone easy on her tonight for some inexplicable reason, but no more.

He pulled away and got to his feet, leaving Sarah on her knees in almost the exact position she'd been when he'd first come in.

"You were doing well until the end," he said coolly, straightening his clothes with shaking hands. "Unfortunately, trying to remove your blindfold was a direct violation of my orders. We'll have to deal with that tomorrow night. You'll receive your instructions at dinner."

He paused, looking down at her. Her beautiful face was turned up towards his. With her eyes covered it was difficult to read her expression.

He was filled with an urge to rip off her blindfold himself and take her into his arms, raining kisses on that soft, sweet mouth.

His hands tightened into fists.

"You can take off the blindfold once I'm gone."

And then he left, without bothering to say goodnight.

CHAPTER 4

As she finished another delicious breakfast, Sarah reflected on the fact that now, at least, she had the answer to one burning question.

She *could* turn Keith Logan on. Last night, she'd literally knocked him on his ass, and it was the sexiest thing that had ever happened to her. Whatever this was to Keith, it wasn't just a game where he pleasured her without taking pleasure himself, staying in absolute control of the situation. He'd lost control a couple of times last night, and she'd never relished anything more in her life.

She wanted to make him lose control again. But he'd made it clear at the end that he didn't want that.

She could understand. She could sympathize. She felt the same way herself . . . or at least, she had until two days ago.

But she was starting to enjoy the experience of not being in control. Well . . . maybe enjoy wasn't the right word. It wasn't like a nice cup of tea, or a rainy day indoors with an Agatha Christie novel.

It was raw. It was intense.

It was dangerous.

Dangerous to the way she'd tried to live her life since she was five years old. Dangerous to her self-imposed isolation. Dangerous to every idea she had about herself.

Keith had pushed her out of her comfort zone, and she felt more exhilarated, more alive, than she ever had before.

And she wanted to give him the same thing. This week they had together was an opportunity. A chance for both of them to step outside the cages they'd made for themselves—cages of loneliness.

Because Keith *was* lonely. She'd never been more certain of anything.

Maybe he'd even been lonely in high school. It seemed inconceivable—he'd always been surrounded by people fawning over him, including every pretty girl at the Academy.

And yet, the only time she'd ever seen him look truly happy had been those moments when he was playing with the headmaster's dog.

She wished she'd had the courage to talk to him back then. He'd given her plenty of openings. He'd always been friendly towards her, but she'd usually responded to his overtures with shrugs or monosyllables, so paralyzed with embarrassment she couldn't even meet his eyes.

Of course a big part of that had been her social anxiety disorder, which hadn't been diagnosed until her freshman year in college. And that wasn't her fault.

Sarah rose from the breakfast table and went to the library, where she wandered slowly around the room, looking at the leather-bound books without really seeing them.

She wouldn't blame herself for the past, but she wasn't a teenage girl anymore. She was a grown woman who saw things differently now, and who could make different decisions.

Another minute brought her to the leather chair in front of the fireplace. She threw herself into it and picked up the phone on the table beside it.

"Hello, Sarah."

Keith sounded almost resigned, as though he'd been expecting—dreading?—her call. Sarah smiled and settled deeper into the chair.

"Did you know I had a crush on you in high school?"

There was a brief, electric silence. "Are you kidding?" he asked after a moment.

"Nope. I'm surprised you don't have a hole in the back of your head, after all the time I spent staring at you in class."

"But you never talked to me in high school. You barely even looked at me."

"I had social anxiety disorder. I still do."

Another silence. How would he react to hearing that? She remembered a friend who'd struggled with bulimia telling her she never revealed that part of her history to men. "Men hate it when women have things wrong with them," she'd said. "Especially weird, psychological things."

Sarah had told her that plenty of men were capable of unconditional love. Of course she'd been speaking from hope, not from experience. For all she knew, her friend might be right.

But she knew in her heart that if she and Keith were going to get to the place she wanted them to be—even if it was only for this one week—then concealment wasn't an option. She had to be willing to show herself to him, and if that meant he rejected her, then so be it.

The silence went on for at least a minute. Then—"I had no idea."

"Neither did I, until a professor of mine in college figured it out and helped me find a good therapist. I've made a lot of progress in the last few years. But that's why it was hard for me to connect with people in high school. Why it's still hard. The truth is, it will probably always be hard. But I'm dealing with it."

"I always knew you were shy, but I didn't realize how much you were struggling. I wish I'd known." There was a pause. "Can I tell you a secret?"

Sarah blinked. "Um . . . sure. Of course."

"I used to make you blush on purpose. I knew if I said hi you would, so even when I knew you probably wouldn't say hi back, sometimes I did it anyway."

She didn't know what to make of that. "You made me blush on purpose?"

"Yeah."

"But . . . why?"

"Because it made you look so beautiful. That pink in your cheeks. It made me wonder what you'd look like blushing all over."

Her breath caught in her throat. Now it was her turn to be silent. She could feel a blush coming on right now, creeping up her chest and her throat and burning in her cheeks.

When Keith spoke again, his voice was low and husky. "In case you haven't figured it out yet, I had a crush on you in high school, too."

No. That wasn't possible. Was it?

"But . . . all those girls. They threw themselves at you. You could have anyone you wanted."

"Anyone but you."

Right, okay. That made a little more sense. "So you wanted me because you couldn't have me? Because I was a challenge?"

"Jesus. No." He paused. "Well . . . maybe a little, at first. But I'm not a fucking idiot. Do you think I couldn't figure out that you were special? That you were the smartest, most interesting girl in school? Even if you wouldn't talk to me, you did have to talk in class every once in a while. And I listened to you. You were passionate and brilliant and you actually gave a shit about things that mattered. How many high school kids can you say that about? I might not have been a prize back then but I give myself this much credit: I've always been able to recognize quality."

He sounded like he meant what he was saying.

He'd liked her in high school?

"I had no idea," she said, unconsciously echoing what he'd said a few minutes before.

She didn't know what to think about this. She couldn't really process it. Once again, everything she'd believed for years was called into question.

And then she heard herself blurt, "I used to watch you all the time. I went to your soccer and basketball games, when I could. You were good, of course. You were good at everything you did. But the only time I ever saw you look happy was when you were with the headmaster's dog."

When he spoke he sounded irritated. "You're obsessed with that damn dog."

That made her smile. "You never did tell me if you ever had a pet."

That brought on the longest silence yet. She had to force herself to stay quiet and let Keith break it when he was ready.

At last he did. "Fine. You want me to say I have a soft spot in my heart for animals? I do. You want me to say I was starved of any real affection growing up, and the only outlet I had was the headmaster's dog? Well, that's true, too. I had a rotten childhood. My mother died when I was a baby and my father was a cold, unfeeling bastard. Is that what you wanted to hear?"

His voice was angry. Really angry. But she'd asked for it, and so she didn't say a word.

"But don't get the idea that I need love now," he went on. "Or that I need to be saved or healed or whatever. I have more money and freedom than most of the human beings on this planet. I have everything I ever wanted." A short silence, and then his voice turned low. "I even got to fuck that pretty mouth of yours last night. So don't worry about me. I'm doing just fine." Another pause. "I'm done talking now, Sarah. If this wasn't enough to satisfy you then I guess you'll pack up and leave. There's nothing I can do about that. But if you stay, you should know that I'm not in the mood to be gentle tonight. But maybe you won't stay to find out just how rough I can be."

He disconnected the call, and for a long time Sarah sat still, without moving. Her skin was tingling.

There was no question she was going to stay.

In spite of what Keith had said, she did think he needed love. But that wasn't the only reason she was staying. The biggest reason was selfish.

She wanted him. There was no part of her that wasn't turned on by Keith Logan, and she wanted everything from him that he was willing to give her—even if it was only for one week.

And even if she was a little bit nervous about tonight.

* * *

Lie face down, naked and blindfolded, and wait for me.

That was it.

Sarah finished reading the letter and tucked it in her back pocket as Nancy brought out dessert. It was caramel custard.

"Mr. Logan said you like this," she said cheerfully.

It was the dessert she'd ordered that night at the restaurant. For a man who wanted to portray himself as cold and aloof, he could be remarkably thoughtful.

"Is he a good boss?" she asked suddenly, as Nancy set the dish down.

Nancy looked a little surprised at the question, but she answered readily enough. "Yes, he is. A wonderful boss."

She probably wouldn't get an answer to her next question, but she asked it anyway.

"Does he . . . have a lot of women over?"

Nancy smiled a little as she poured more espresso into Sarah's cup. "I shouldn't talk about that."

"Of course not. I'm sorry. I—"

"I shouldn't, but I will."

Sarah blinked.

"I've been with him five years, and yes, he's been with his share of women. And yes, sometimes they stay the night. But he's never had a woman living here."

She shouldn't be so happy to hear that—but she was.

"I'm not exactly living here. I mean . . . I'm only here for a week."

"Mmm."

She wasn't sure how to interpret that, but she figured she'd put Nancy on the spot enough for one night.

Lie face down, naked and blindfolded, and wait for me.

She'd followed instructions and was now lying on her bed as tense as a bowstring. She tried not to wonder what was coming. Everything they'd done so far she'd loved, but of course that was no guarantee she'd feel that way tonight.

She had to remember that no matter how drawn she was to Keith, how much she wanted to stay, if something happened she didn't like she could end it and walk away.

The door opened.

Her heart thumped as she listened to Keith crossing the room towards her. Then she felt the bed give as he sat on the edge beside her.

"Lay on my lap," he said, his voice cool and even.

Shit. Shit. Did this mean he was going to spank her, or something? Of course that was one of the possibilities that had occurred to her when she read his note, but she'd let herself hope that it wouldn't happen.

Maybe it wouldn't hurt very much. Maybe—

"Now." His voice was like a whip, and she knew she had to decide.

She rose up on her knees and moved towards him on the bed. She used her hands to feel where he was and then awkwardly laid herself down across his powerful thighs.

He was bare-chested but he was wearing pants—jeans, she thought. The denim was rough against her skin, and she felt an unexpected jolt of excitement.

Keith ran his big palm along her spine and down across her backside. He traced the curves of her buttocks with slow, gentle strokes, and suddenly she realized something.

She liked this. She liked lying naked and vulnerable on Keith's lap, blindfolded and at his mercy.

Something was happening to her spine. She was lying still, not moving, but it felt like she was almost . . . undulating.

Surrendering.

"You have a beautiful ass, Sarah."

Then he lifted his hand and brought it down on her bottom with an audible crack.

She gasped, but more from surprise than pain. It stung—no question about that—but it didn't really hurt. Still, as adrenaline coursed through her body, instinct made her squirm away from him.

Instantly he caught her wrists and bound them together behind her back, using something that felt like the tie of a robe. He must have had it ready.

Oh, God. What was wrong with her that she felt so excited right now? In a burst of clarity she realized that, on some level, she'd been telling herself this side of Keith was something she was putting up with in order to be with him. Like it was a flaw she had to accept.

But the truth was, she wanted this as much as he did. She loved everything they'd done together so far, and she wanted more.

"You're not going anywhere," he said in the low, sexy voice she adored.

When she struggled this time it wasn't instinct—it was because she wanted to. She wanted to feel how hopeless it was, how completely Keith could dominate her.

He held her down easily with a hand on her lower back.

"You were doing so well," he said, using his other hand to stroke her bare bottom again. The soft caress made her skin tighten everywhere, as though it were too small for her body. "And then you had to try and take your blindfold off. You should know better, Sarah. I make the rules at night."

Was he going to spank her again? She held her breath in anticipation, but he just kept stroking her.

"If you're a good girl, we won't have to do this again—even if your ass does look fucking amazing with the mark of my hand on it. But I'm willing to move on if you've learned your lesson. Have you?"

He was letting her off the hook. With one spank, he was letting her off the hook.

He thought she couldn't take it. He thought she didn't really like this. He'd talked about how rough he could be, and now he was backing off.

"No."

Keith's hand went still. "What?"

Her heart was pounding. "I said no. I haven't learned my lesson. I think . . ." She swallowed. "I think you should make sure I have."

The silence was so electric it seemed to crackle across her skin.

Then she felt his erection. The heat and hardness seemed to burn through his jeans. She remembered holding all that masculine power in her hands and her mouth last night, and a shiver went through her.

Keith's hand drifted slowly over her ass, paused, and then moved down between her legs. She wanted to part them further, but she couldn't seem to move. When he found the wetness there his hand went still again.

"Sarah," he said, his voice shaken.

There was no warning before the next spanking. This one was a little harder, but there was so much more pleasure than pain.

"Apparently you're a much naughtier girl than I realized. I think you need a lesson in which one of us has the upper hand."

When he said the word *hand* his came down again. The sting was like an electric shock, and she jumped and wriggled in his lap, feeling a pulse of excitement when she rubbed against the bulge in his jeans.

His hand came down again and again, raining sharp blows on her burning skin until it was almost too much.

Just before it was too much, he stopped. "Who's in charge here, Sarah?"

"You are," she gasped, and a delicious feeling swept through her when she said the words. Her ass was on fire and the burn spread all through her.

He untied her hands and shifted her off his lap, laying her on her back and reaching for her wrists. In seconds she was cuffed to the bed, the hot, tender skin of her backside rubbing against the silk comforter.

Keith slid one hand underneath to palm her bottom and laid the other across her damp pussy. The part of her that ached and throbbed was trapped between those strong hands, and even though she tried to stay still she twitched spasmodically in near-frantic desire.

Keith chuckled as he bent close to whisper in her ear. "Who's the master here?"

"You are."

The hand on her bottom moved so he could dip one finger into her honeyed wetness. Then she felt that slick finger at her anus.

She tensed up, and he chuckled again. "I think you want me everywhere, Sarah. I think you'll let me go anywhere I want to."

The hand on her pussy shifted, and she felt two fingers probing at her entrance, not penetrating yet but poised to do just that.

If she moved as much as a millimeter, he'd be inside her. She held herself still.

Then her breath whooshed out of her in a gasp as the finger at her anus pushed inside to the first knuckle.

She arched off the bed, and the movement thrust her onto the fingers at her pussy. When she tried to retreat from that invasion she impaled herself further on the finger in her ass.

The more she tried to get away the more she was invaded.

"Keith!"

As soon as she cried out his name she remembered that she was supposed to call him Sir, but he didn't say anything about it. A sound came from him, something between a groan and a growl.

"Take it deeper."

Oh, God. His words drove her over the edge and in the next instant she was rocking against him, shamelessly fucking his fingers on both ends. The friction inside her made her burn until every inch of her was on fire.

Then, suddenly, his fingers were gone. She opened her mouth to cry out in protest, but then she heard his zipper and the sound of foil ripping.

Her heart slammed against her chest. *Please, please, please, please...*

He shoved her legs roughly apart and gripped her hips.

"You're mine," he said, and pleasure exploded inside her as he drove his cock inside her, to the hilt.

He was so much bigger than the other guy she'd been with. He was so big she felt split in two. How could she contain so much?

When he started to move, it wasn't like his fingers. This was a true invasion. He was so long and thick it hurt just a little.

She wanted to hurt like this for the rest of her life. She wanted Keith inside her, possessing her, filling all her empty places. She wanted the friction, the heat and hardness, the big hands moving to her thighs, forcing her legs wider apart as he pushed inside her again and again.

She wanted those dominating thrusts telling her who she belonged to.

You're mine.

She was helpless under the onslaught. Her wrists were cuffed. Her legs were pinioned under his hands, her legs spread wide as he fucked her relentlessly, deliberately, thoroughly.

Then his angle shifted, and he was bumping against her clit with every flex of his hips. There was a roaring in her ears as the tension built to dizzying heights, her body like an elastic that had been pulled too tight.

And then she broke.

She was splintered by ecstasy, every cell in her body separately exploding.

Keith stayed deep inside her during her orgasm, grinding himself against her until the aftershocks rose suddenly into a second climax.

Her body was buzzing and quivering when he pulled out and slammed into her again, his thrusts harder and rougher than before. He pounded her mercilessly until she felt his cock pulse inside her, and then he called out her name as he shuddered with his own orgasm.

His weight collapsed on top of her, and for the first time she wished her hands weren't cuffed. She wanted to stroke his back, his shoulders, his hair.

Instead she lay still and basked in the feeling of his big body pinning hers to the mattress. He rested his head on her shoulder, and she let herself enjoy that, too.

"Sarah," he said after what seemed like a long, long time.

"Yes?" she whispered.

He shifted his head and pressed a kiss to her collarbone. "There's a possibility that you and I are sexually compatible."

A bubble of warmth and laughter rose inside her.

"Could be," she said gravely, wishing she could see his face but not asking this time.

They lay in silence for a while after that—a remarkably companionable silence.

It occurred to her that she couldn't remember ever feeling this relaxed with another human being.

Apparently the trick was to be tied down, blindfolded, and fucked senseless.

Another bubble of laughter rose, taking shape in a smile.

Keith finally eased himself to the side. "I'm sorry—I must have been heavy," he said, trailing a hand down her body from her neck to her waist.

"I liked it," she said simply, and then gasped when his hand covered her mound.

"Just staking out my territory," he said softly.

"You can't start anything now. My bones are already melted."

"I'm not starting anything," he said, the hint of a smile in his voice. "I just want to touch you."

"Well, I am in handcuffs. You can pretty much do anything you want."

"I like the sound of that."

His hand moved lazily upwards, across her belly to her breasts. He cupped one and leaned over to kiss the other.

"You have the most perfect breasts I've ever seen."

She couldn't let that pass—not when she thought about the women he must have been with over the years. "Oh, please."

"You don't believe me?"

"I most certainly do not."

He shifted so his hands covered both breasts, and her nipples pebbled into diamonds.

He pinched them hard. "Who's the master here?"

"You are," she gasped.

He pinched tighter. "Who has the most perfect breasts I've ever seen?"

"I do!"

"That's my girl," he said, and let her go.

My girl.

She bit her lip, telling herself not to hope.

But it wasn't possible. Despite all her efforts, hope took up residence in her heart.

Was there a chance that they could have more than this week? Or were the boundaries he'd drawn for them too thick?

She opened her mouth to speak and then closed it again. She couldn't have this conversation with a blindfold on.

She wasn't sure she could have this conversation at all.

But as though Keith had sensed her unspoken words, he reached up to release her cuffs.

The spell between them was broken.

"You can take off the blindfold after I'm gone."

And a minute later, he was.

CHAPTER 5

He'd managed to make it into the office today, but he'd skipped all his meetings. Now he was sitting at his desk with his head in his hands.

He was going to call off their deal. But he couldn't tell Sarah the real reason. He'd say he had to go out of the country, but since she'd honored her side of the bargain, the painting would still be hers.

The memory of last night flashed into his mind again, and he groaned.

The real reason he had to end it was that it mattered too much.

She mattered too much. And it was starting to mess with his head.

He looked up, and his eyes fell on the reproduction of *Nighthawks*.

The painting had been done in 1942. It showed a diner late at night with three customers, a man sitting on his own and a couple sitting together. The guy behind the counter was talking to the couple.

Sarah had asked him why that painting was his favorite, and he hadn't answered her.

He'd seen the painting for the first time when he was eleven or twelve, and even back then he'd identified with the man sitting on his own. He didn't look unhappy or lonely, or anything like that. He looked cool and solitary and complete within himself.

He looked content.

Now his eyes moved to the couple. They looked relaxed and easy, like they'd been together a long time.

They looked happy.

For the first time, he wondered what it would be like to identify with the man in the couple instead of the man sitting alone.

At two o'clock in the afternoon, Valerie knocked on the door. Without waiting for an invitation to enter, she came in with a big brown box in her arms.

"A messenger just dropped this off for you," she said.

He frowned at her. She was grinning, which was never a good sign. "Yeah? What is it?"

In answer she set the box down on the floor, and jumping, cavorting, galumphing out of it came a Jack Russell terrier.

His jaw dropped.

He knew immediately who'd done this. There was only one person in the entire world who would have done this.

Sarah Harper had gotten him a puppy.

He couldn't move. He just sat there, staring, as the puppy explored the office with over-the-top enthusiasm, discovering his existence after a few minutes with a frenzy of delight.

The puppy was too small to jump up on his lap, but that didn't stop him from trying.

After about thirty seconds of sitting there, frozen, while the small bundle of fur scrabbled at his pants and made eager, frantic puppy sounds, he gave in. He reached down and picked him up, holding him close enough to be slathered in sloppy kisses.

"My God," Valerie said in hushed tones. "Who are you, and what have you done with my boss?"

"I can't believe she did this," he murmured, setting the squirming puppy back down on the floor.

"Who?"

"Sarah Harper."

Valerie stared at him. "The one in the portrait?"

"Yeah. I knew her in high school and we . . . uh . . . reconnected this week."

Valerie raised her eyebrows. "I see."

She was eloquently silent after that, and Keith frowned at her.

"Wipe that grin off your face."

"I will not."

He looked away from her to watch the Jack Russell tear around the room. After a minute he paused to water a potted plant in the corner before charging off to attack a wastebasket.

"Did you see that? He peed in my office. That little monster just peed in my office."

He realized he was grinning, too, when he met Valerie's eyes again.

"I'll alert the cleaning company," she said. "So why did Sarah Harper get you a puppy?"

A tide of warmth rose up in him. "She wanted to make me happy."

"And did she?"

He couldn't seem to stop smiling. "Yeah, she did." He paused for a moment. "She does."

* * *

Sarah was sitting at her favorite desk in the library. Her computer was open in front of her, but she wasn't working. She was staring into space and thinking about Keith.

The messenger service had confirmed they had delivered the puppy an hour ago, but she hadn't heard from him.

She'd obviously made a mistake.

If he didn't want the dog, she would take him. Her landlord allowed pets.

If he didn't want her, that would be harder. But she'd just have to accept it.

And she did have a few more days with him . . . unless she'd messed everything up by going too far. Getting too personal. Breaking the rules.

She heard the library door opening, and she turned to see if Nancy was coming in.

But it wasn't Nancy. It was Keith. He stood in the doorway staring at her, and her body went hot all over, just like that day at the museum.

She hadn't seen him since the night they had dinner. She'd been blindfolded during every encounter with him. She'd heard his voice, she'd felt his touch, but she hadn't seen his face.

It felt shocking to see it now. To see him, and to see him looking at her. Somehow, she felt more naked than she had in his arms last night.

"You got me a puppy," he said after a moment.

She nodded slowly. "I did."

"If I'd wanted a puppy, I could have gotten one myself."

Her heart was pounding. "Sometimes people need a push."

His blue eyes lasered into hers. "Maybe they do." There was a short silence, and then he went on. "A puppy requires a lot of attention."

"Yes."

"What'll happen when I'm out of the country on business?"

"Um . . . Nancy?"

"I don't want to put more work on Nancy's plate."

She tilted her head to the side. "Rumor has it you're fairly well off. I bet you could hire someone to look after your dog while you're on business trips."

"You can't hire affection, which is what puppies need. I can't pay someone to love him the way I do."

Her heart turned over. "You love that puppy? But you just met him."

"I know it's soon. But that's what's in my heart." He took a step towards her. "I was hoping maybe you would help me out. We could share custody."

Her breath caught in her chest, and it was a minute before she could speak. "That would mean staying in each other's lives. Even after the week is over."

He nodded, his eyes never leaving hers. "That's what I want. If it's something you want."

She swallowed. "It is."

He took another step towards her. "Maybe you should think about it first. You'd be taking on a lot, Sarah. The puppy isn't house trained yet—and neither am I."

She smiled at him. "It won't be hard to train the puppy. Jack Russells are smart. As for you . . ." She paused. "I wouldn't change a thing. I like you exactly the way you are."

His eyes lit up, and she saw him take a deep breath. Then he crossed the room in a few long strides and took her in his arms, bending her back in a kiss that took her breath away.

When he finally broke away she was gasping.

"You're so beautiful," he whispered, framing her face in his hands and gazing at her. "It was torture staring at that portrait every day at the museum, knowing I'd never have the real thing. A part of me still can't believe this is real. That you're here, with me. Wanting to be with me."

"I want you to keep the portrait."

That took him aback. "But it's yours. I mean . . . it should be yours."

She shook her head. "I don't need it. I wanted it because it reminded me of my father, and because it gave me the illusion that we were connected."

She took a breath. "I loved my father, but we weren't connected. That takes work . . . and courage. My father and I had neither."

"But that painting . . ."

"It was always easy for my father to see people through his art. I think he did see me when he painted that portrait, and I'm grateful we had that, at least. But I'm looking for a different kind of connection now. The kind that's not at a safe distance."

His eyes searched hers. "What kind of connection are you looking for?"

"Something messy and human and scary. Something real."

He slid his arms around her waist. "I think I can offer you that."

"Good."

"I just want to be sure you understand . . ."

"What?"

"What I like in the bedroom—it's a part of who I am. That's not going to change."

"God, I hope not."

He took a step back and smiled at her. "You mean that?"

"Hell, yes."

"Then take off your clothes."

He was still smiling at her, but a wicked gleam had come into his eyes.

Goose bumps swept across her skin. "It's, um, daytime."

"Yes."

"Nancy could walk in, or Paul—"

"I sent them home. We're alone in the house."

She took a deep breath and let it out. She'd thought from the beginning that her being blindfolded had made Keith feel safe, and it probably had. But it had made her feel safe, too.

She couldn't move.

"Scared?" he asked softly.

She nodded.

"Too bad." He took another step back and folded his arms. "Do it now."

A shiver went through her, but she knew Keith wasn't kidding. When it came to sex, he gave the orders. She could follow them or go home.

Her choice.

She reached for the hem of her tee shirt and pulled it up over her head. Then she reached behind her for the clasp on her bra and undid it, letting it fall to the ground.

"Nice," Keith said, moving close enough that he could cover her breasts with his hands. Her hardening nipples poked into his palms.

"Lose the pants," he instructed, and she kicked off her sandals before tugging her jeans and panties down.

In a few seconds she stood naked in front of Keith Logan.

"Even nicer," he said, and she could see the desire in his eyes—the expression she'd only imagined before. "Now go to the desk and bend over."

A flutter of excitement made her knees weak, but she made it to the desk without collapsing. Then she rested her forearms on the table as she bent at the waist.

"Spread your legs wider," he said, and as she did she heard the sound of his zipper.

She bit her lip as moisture flooded her core. Then Keith put one hand on her hip and used the other to stroke her.

"You're wet," he murmured, and then he landed a sharp spank on her bottom.

Adrenaline spiked in her bloodstream, and now she was even wetter.

"Do you want me?" he asked roughly, and she started to say yes. But then she shook her head. "No."

His hands tightened on her and she knew her answer had surprised and excited him.

"I think you're lying, Sarah. You've been thinking about me all day, haven't you? Thinking about my cock inside you."

"No," she said again, and he spanked her twice more.

"It doesn't matter if you want me or not. I'm going to fuck you and there's nothing you can do about it."

Because she loved to feel his strength she used her hands to push against the desk, trying to straighten up.

But he was too fast for her. He caught her wrists and twisted them behind her back, and then he tied them with—what was that?

His belt. She didn't know why that was so sexy, but it was.

With her hands bound she was almost helpless. Still she kept struggling even when Keith held her down easily with one hand on her back, pressing her breasts against the cool wood of the desk.

Then she felt the tip of his cock against her sopping entrance.

"Do you want me?" he asked again, rougher than before.

"No!" she cried out, even as her body quivered with eagerness.

Then he pushed inside her, slow and deliberate, while he used the fingers of one hand to massage her clit.

She was trapped between his cock and his fingers, and she found herself pushing back and then forward, delicious sensation waiting for her everywhere. She moaned.

Keith bent over her and whispered in her ear. "You need this hard cock, don't you?"

Her role fell away and the truth slipped out. "Yes . . . oh, God, yes . . ."

He fucked her harder, deeper, and his fingers on her clit moved faster.

"You'll let me fuck you whenever I want to."

"Yes..."

"Tell me who you belong to."

"You!"

"That's my girl," he growled, and then he was pounding her so hard and fast she couldn't form a thought, much less a word—except for his name.

"Keith!" she cried out, climaxing in a fevered rush as her muscles clamped around him, milking his cock until he came, too.

The only sound in the room was the ragged gasp of their breath and the pounding of their hearts.

After the hurricane in her body died down she became aware that Keith was nuzzling the back of her neck. She arched into him, and he undid the belt around her wrists. Then he pulled her upright and spun her so they were face to face.

He slid his hands into her hair and kissed her, and she wrapped her arms around him as she kissed him back with everything in her heart—even the things she hadn't said yet.

She didn't feel in a rush to speak the words. When the time was right, she wouldn't be able to hold them back.

The kiss ended, and she pulled back to look at him. He was smiling, and something in his eyes told her he already knew what she was still too shy to say.

HIS ONE DESIRE

CHAPTER 1

This couldn't be happening.

But as Kali Jones stared across her desk into her boss's face, hoping to find some evidence that he was joking, all she saw was the blissful happiness of a basic cable TV producer who's been approached by one of Hollywood's rising stars about the network's newest project.

Except it wasn't just any project. It was *her* project. The paranormal drama she'd dreamed of doing for years, and which had finally been given the green light by the network.

Because of her budget and also because of her vision for the show, Kali had been planning to cast unknowns. And even if they'd been able to afford a big star, Luke Tanner was the last actor in the world she'd ever want to work with.

Once upon a time, she and Luke been friends—before they'd become enemies. Of course he had no idea that Kali Jones, writer and director of *Ghosts*, was Caroline Jones, the girl he'd known back in high school. When he found out, he wouldn't want anything to do with the show.

But Kali didn't want things to get that far. She didn't want Luke to find out who she was, and she didn't want to see him ever again. Which meant she had to nip this in the bud right now.

She took a deep breath and prepared to fight, both for her show and for her peace of mind.

"Tom, I thought we'd agreed to cast fresh faces. Not only because of our budget constraints but also because—"

"But that's the best part! According to his agent, Luke Tanner is so excited about *Ghosts* that he's willing to work for what we're able to pay."

She felt a sudden chill. "Did his agent happen to mention why he's so interested in this project?"

Tom grinned the grin of a man who was sure he was about to impart good news. "As a matter of fact, he did. Luke wants to work with *you*, Kali. He saw *Negative Space* and loved it, and he wants to work on *Ghosts* because you're writing and directing it. What do you think of *that*?" he finished triumphantly.

Another chill swept through her, leaving her palms clammy and her stomach nauseous.

"Well?" Tom prompted after a moment, obviously puzzled that Kali wasn't bouncing up and down with excitement. "Isn't that amazing?"

"Amazing," she echoed faintly.

So it wasn't a coincidence. Luke knew who she was. He knew, and he'd deliberately set up this situation.

For one brief moment she considered telling Tom the truth about why Luke wanted to work with her, but she rejected the idea almost immediately. Even if she gave him the whole story, which she'd rather die than do, Tom would never believe that Luke Tanner—rich, successful, and on his way to becoming one of Hollywood's biggest stars—would go to this much trouble to get revenge for something that had happened before he was famous, when he was a teenage boy from a poor family.

But Tom didn't know Luke. When Luke had a goal in his sights, he pursued it with relentless drive. People usually ended up giving him whatever he wanted.

Apparently, he hadn't forgotten or forgiven the one person who hadn't.

Kali ran her hands through her short dark hair and tried to think clearly. She had to stop this somehow. Luke didn't really want to be a part of *Ghosts*. He'd involve himself in the show to the extent required to ruin it, and then he'd walk away.

But she wasn't about to let that happen. She'd invested too much of herself in this project to let Luke's petty desire for revenge destroy it.

She took another breath. "I know you're excited right now, but making a casting decision like this would go against everything we've talked about. And it's not just the money. We want to work with unknown actors so we don't have associations from past roles. We want to do something fresh, where we can take risks and experiment and fly under the radar for a while."

Tom stared at her like she was some odd species of alien. "I know the plan was to be creative on a small budget, but we'd be insane to turn down an opportunity like this. With Luke Tanner on board we won't *have* to be creative on a small budget. We can be creative on a *big* budget."

His eyes glowed. "When the network execs get wind of this they'll write us a blank check. Remember all those weeks you spent figuring out how to produce the special effects you wanted with no money? Well, now you won't have to. Your job just got easier, my friend."

Kali couldn't look at Tom anymore. She stared down at her desk instead, fixing her eyes on the framed playbill from the off-Broadway production of *Negative Space*. They hadn't had much money for that project, either, and Kali had never been more proud of a show in her life. Didn't Tom remember the satisfaction of making something out of nothing?

Apparently he didn't. Apparently the money and spotlight that would come attached to Luke Tanner were things he desperately wanted. Which meant it wouldn't be any use to tell him she didn't really want her job to get easier. That she'd always done her best work with limited resources.

She had one hand in her lap, and now she clenched it into a fist. She'd have to find another way to convince Tom.

"Luke is Hollywood's golden boy right now. He doesn't really want to come to New York to do a TV show. This is just a whim—a whim he'll never follow through on. He'll disrupt everything we've been doing, and then he'll go back to L.A. where he belongs. But by then it might be too late for us to recover."

Tom frowned. "That possibility did occur to me, Kali. I'm not a complete idiot. I had a very frank discussion with Luke's agent on this very subject, as a matter of fact. He told me that the best way for us to get Luke's signature on a contract is if you meet with him one-on-one. To woo him, as Quentin put it."

Bile rose in her throat. So that was Luke's plan—to humiliate her by putting her into a situation where she'd have to *woo* him. God, how he'd love that—to be the one with all the power, holding all the cards, while she was the humble supplicant.

"No way." She was startled to hear herself—she sounded almost angry.

Tom looked startled, too. Kali never got angry.

"Kali—"

"I won't do it."

"But, Kali—"

She folded her arms and tried to look fierce and implacable, like a heroine from one of her shows. She'd always written women who were stronger than she was, and she'd always hoped that some of their toughness would rub off on their creator.

"I'm not going to beg Luke Tanner to work with us. Especially when I don't want him to."

Tom took a deep breath and let it out slowly. "In that case, you should know that I'm probably going to lose my job."

Her arms dropped to her sides. "What? What are you talking about?"

"Three of my five shows are missing their ratings marks. Diane gave me the straight word last week. They'll give me until the end of this year, and if things haven't started to turn around by then, I'll get the axe."

He sounded matter of fact, but Kali knew that his partner had been laid off a few months before and that

Tom was supporting both of them while Andrew looked for another job.

She slumped back in her chair. "If they fire you, they'll probably let me go, too. We'll look for a new gig together. We could—"

Tom shook his head. "They're not going to let you go, Kali. They love the writing you're doing for *Roommates*." *Roommates* was the network's highest rated show. "For that alone they'd keep you on. You have a big future at this network."

She thought about what he hadn't said. "But *Ghosts*?"

It was Tom's turn to sigh. "You know they weren't sure about *Ghosts* to begin with, and there's a chance it'll never air. But if we could get a star like Luke Tanner on board . . . well, that would be a whole new ballgame. I guarantee you they'd get behind us one hundred percent."

Her eyes fell to the framed playbill again. When their meager funds for *Negative Space* had run out, Tom had put up five thousand dollars of his own money to keep the production alive. And a few years later, he'd helped her make it into a movie.

"Okay," she said, hopelessly. This was doomed to end badly, but she couldn't say no to Tom. Maybe she could manage the Luke problem without too much damage. Maybe she could—

Tom was talking again, the happy look back in his eyes. "Wonderful! I knew I could count on you. Luke's coming into town next week, so we'll set up a meeting for—"

The intercom buzzed, and the two of them heard the receptionist's voice.

"Ms. Jones? You have a visitor."

She glanced at her desk calendar to confirm that she didn't have any appointments for this afternoon. "Who is it, Stella?"

"Luke Tanner," Stella said. There was suppressed excitement in her voice despite the fact that she'd seen her fair share of celebrities over the years.

Kali froze. "I thought you said he was coming next week," she hissed to Tom. "Didn't you say next week?"

Tom shrugged. "That's what his agent said, but I guess he flew out early." Before she could stop him, Tom leaned over her desk and spoke into the intercom. "Stella, this is Tom. Have someone bring Luke up to Kali's office, will you?"

"I'll bring him up myself," she said, her voice bubbling.

Of course you will.

Kali sprang to her feet, grabbing her purse from the back of her chair. "I'll be right back," she said to Tom. "I—I need to go to the ladies room."

She was out the door before he could say a word, half running down the hall to the bathroom.

She didn't have much time. She turned on the cold water and splashed her face, patting her skin dry with paper towels before fishing in her purse for the few items of makeup she possessed—under-eye concealer, blush, lip gloss. She applied those with shaking hands and then ran a brush through her hair.

She stuffed everything back into her purse and glanced in the mirror. She'd put on too much blush, so she grabbed another paper towel and rubbed most of it off. Her khaki pants and navy blue button down shirt were both wrinkled, but she'd have to live with that.

Not that she cared what Luke thought of her appearance. She didn't. It was just that she would prefer to present the most professional image possible when meeting with a Hollywood star, no matter who it was. She owed it to the network. She owed it to Tom. She—

Had to go right now if she wanted to be back behind her desk before Luke got there. She jerked open the bathroom door and charged down the hall, turning the corner that led to her office and crashing into someone with a chest like a brick wall.

She was knocked off-balance, but strong hands caught her before she fell.

"Oh God, I'm so sorry, I—"

Then she looked up and saw who she'd crashed into. It was Luke Tanner, his big hands gripping her shoulders and his eyes hidden behind aviator glasses.

An electric feeling went through her. She'd forgotten what she was saying, which was probably just as well. She wasn't sure she could speak coherently right now.

"Ms. Jones, are you all right?"

It was Stella, peering at her from behind Luke. Tom, looking startled, was standing in the doorway of her office.

"Of course," she said, her voice coming out as a croak. She started to pull away from Luke, and when his hands didn't immediately loosen she jerked out of his grasp in a panicked spasm, stumbling back a few steps.

"Mr. Tanner, I'm Tom Hammond," Tom said smoothly, coming forward to offer a hand. "And this is our writer and director, Kali Jones."

Her boss frowned at her, his eyes sending a clear message. *Pull yourself together.*

He was right. She needed to get a grip.

Luke shook Tom's hand with a smile. "It's a pleasure, Tom—and please call me Luke." Then he turned to Kali.

"It's nice to meet you," she managed.

This was the moment of truth. Tom's introduction had made it obvious she hadn't told anyone they'd met before. Would Luke go along with that, or would he expose her?

"It's nice to meet you, too, Ms. Jones."

A rush of relief made her feel lightheaded. Then she saw the quirk at the corner of his mobile, sensual mouth, and her heart sank. This was only a short reprieve. Whatever Luke had in store for her, it wasn't anything good.

She wondered what he was planning.

And then, suddenly, she felt a stirring of anger. "Why are you wearing those glasses?" she heard herself ask. "In case you hadn't noticed, we're indoors. I think your retinas are safe from UV rays in here."

In the moment of astonished silence that followed her words, Kali was just as surprised as anyone else.

Tom was the first to speak. "I think Kali wants a look at those famous baby blues of yours, Luke. What did *People* say when you were in their list of sexiest men?"

"They said he redefined the term 'bedroom eyes'," Stella chimed in eagerly.

"Well," Luke said after a moment, "if Ms. Jones wants to see my eyes, I'd hate to disappoint her."

She looked up just as Luke swept off his shades, revealing the cobalt blue eyes that so many women swooned over.

Her stomach muscles tightened.

It wasn't just the eyes that made women swoon, she admitted reluctantly. It was the whole package. His hard-as-a-rock body, encased in worn jeans, a white tee shirt, and his signature black leather jacket. His chiseled features and dark blond hair. And most of all that cocky half grin, that grin that said he was up for anything and looking for trouble.

As she stared at him that grin got even wider, and she felt her own mouth tightening in response. Every other woman in America might dream about his smile, but she didn't.

"Well, Luke," Tom said after a short pause. "Why don't we go into Kali's office?"

"Sounds good."

It was a relief to turn away from him, a relief to go into her office and sit behind her cluttered desk again. This was her place of power. This was where she wrote and edited scripts, where she talked to actors and production staff. She let the worn leather chair cradle her body in comforting familiarity and willed herself to calm down.

"Can I bring you anything to drink, Mr. Tanner?" Stella asked breathlessly, hovering in the doorway.

He grinned that grin at her. "No thanks, Stella. And please call me Luke."

"All right . . . Luke." She said the name like a benediction, and Kali rolled her eyes.

Tom shot her a glare that would have leveled a grizzly at twenty paces. *Cut it out,* he mouthed at her.

Luke turned back to face them. He took off his jacket and slung it over the back of his chair, revealing the powerful arms and shoulders that made him such a draw in those big budget action films. Then he stretched his legs out in front of him, crossing one booted foot over the other and sliding his hands into the pockets of his jeans. The movement made his biceps bunch and his tee shirt strain across his chest.

In spite of herself, Kali felt a tingling rush as she watched him.

That's just biology, she told herself, ashamed of the way her body responded to the blatant masculinity on display.

Women were hard-wired to look for a strong alpha male to mate with, as the best way to ensure the survival of the species. It was only that atavistic strain in her DNA that caused her nerves to flutter when she looked at Luke. He practically radiated strength and power—tall and broad and muscular, with an unmistakable aura of money and success. It was only natural for her body to want to mate with him. Her cavewoman ancestors would undoubtedly have done so.

But she wasn't a cavewoman. She was a woman in the twenty-first century, strong and competent in her own right. And she would *not* fall under the spell of Luke Tanner's sexual magnetism.

"Tom and I were under the impression that you were coming into town next week," she said evenly.

"That was the plan," he said, smiling at her and then at Tom, who sat in the other visitor's chair. "But when Quentin—my agent—said that you'd responded favorably to my interest in *Ghosts*, I just couldn't wait. I got on a plane this morning, and here I am."

"I can't tell you how flattered we are," Tom said, very close to gushing.

Kali's hands, in her lap and out of sight, clenched into fists. "Flattered and surprised," she said, trying to keep her voice neutral. "I must admit, Mr. Tanner, I can't imagine why a star of your caliber would be interested in a TV show—especially a TV show that films in New York. It doesn't seem like a good career move for you."

"A career isn't just an upward trajectory," Luke said. "It's also working on projects you're excited about—with people you're excited to work with."

Tom seemed ready to genuflect. "The feeling is totally mutual, Luke. We couldn't be more pleased by your interest, and we're willing to do whatever it takes to make you a part of this show."

"Is that true, Ms. Jones?" Luke asked softly, a wicked gleam in his blue eyes as he leaned towards her. "Are you willing to do whatever it takes?"

And so the humiliation begins, she thought, her skin prickling with trepidation. She stared back at him with what she hoped was a cool smile.

"I always do whatever it takes to make my shows the best they can be, Mr. Tanner."

"Call me Luke."

"Luke." She said the name reluctantly, and he smiled a little as he leaned back in his chair.

"What I really want is to hear more about your vision for the show, Kali. Maybe over dinner tonight?"

"I can't. I have plans." God, how glad she was to be able to say that.

Luke's eyes narrowed a little. "Tomorrow, then."

She shook her head, trying to keep herself from smiling in satisfaction. "I'm leaving tomorrow for the network's annual retreat. Tom's going, too. We'll both be gone this weekend, and we won't be back until Tuesday." She paused. "I'm sure you don't want to wait around in the city for us, Luke. You'll probably want to head back to L.A. Why don't we give you a call sometime next week? We could set up a video conference so you don't have to fly all the way out here again."

"That's very thoughtful of you," he said. "Have you always been this considerate of other peoples' time?"

She flushed. Suddenly unable to meet his eyes, she turned to Tom, who was frowning at her.

"I'm sure for something as important as this, the network would understand if you want to skip the—"

She shook her head again. "No, I can't possibly get out of it. I'm giving two presentations, remember? And we're doing the story conference for *Roommates* on Monday. We're going to map out the arc for next season. I can't miss that."

Tom looked ready to argue with her, but Luke spoke up first. "Next week will be fine for me. I have a lot of friends and colleagues in New York I'd like to connect with while I'm here. I won't have any trouble keeping busy while you two are away, and we can pick up our discussion when you get back."

Tom's face lit up with relief. "That's incredibly accommodating of you, Luke."

"Hey, no problem. I'm the one who showed up out of nowhere, right? I had no reason to expect that you'd be available on such short notice." He rose to his feet, causing Tom to leap to his.

"It was great to meet you," Luke said, shaking the other man's hand before turning to her. "Would you be willing to walk me out, Kali? I'm afraid I might get lost in this rabbit warren of a building." He smiled amiably.

Crap. There was no way she could get out of it without open rudeness, and she'd already crossed that line once. If she did it again Tom would probably have a heart attack.

She took a deep breath. Maybe she could use this to her advantage. If they had a minute alone in the elevator, she could tell him in no uncertain terms that if he'd come here to mess with her she'd make him regret it. She'd built a life here in New York, and she wasn't about to let him destroy it.

"I'd be delighted," she said, smiling back at him sweetly.

CHAPTER 2

It was a damn good thing he was a trained actor. He was acting his ass off right now, playing the role of a man who didn't give a fuck that he was within touching distance of the only woman who'd ever broken his heart—and who could still make him feel the hollow ache of helpless need.

Helpless was not the way he wanted to feel. He'd felt that enough as a kid, and once he was on his own he swore he'd never feel helpless again. He'd make so much money that it would no longer be a possibility. Money was power, and he would never be without power again.

His plan had been a success. The world was his oyster now, his childhood of struggle and poverty so far behind him it wasn't even a blip in his rear view mirror.

His past was past—with one exception. The woman who was walking beside him right now, scowling when other women popped up from their desks to gawk at him.

"You've got to lay this shit to rest," his oldest friend had told him. They'd been playing one-on-one basketball in the gym, and Luke had paused to sink a three-pointer before asking him what he meant.

Joe went to the bleachers to sit, wiping the sweat off his face with a hand towel. "Caroline Jones. You've got to lay her to rest."

Luke stiffened, staring at him. "What are you talking about?"

"She's still fucking you up, man."

"Like hell she is. I haven't thought about her in a decade."

"Yeah, you have," Joe said. "She's the reason you broke up with Maria. She's the reason you break up with all your girlfriends."

A strange sliver of panic pierced him. "That's crazy. Caroline Jones is just some girl I knew in high school. She doesn't have any power over me now."

"Yeah, she does. But it doesn't have to be that way. You should go see her, man. Conquer the past. Capture her spirit."

Joe had a Hopi grandfather, and occasionally he came out with pseudo-spiritual pronouncements that drove Luke nuts. "Capture her spirit? What the hell does that mean?"

"It means you need to take your power back. Personally, I think you should do it by fucking her. I think your whole problem is that you never did fuck her, so there's this whole mystery aspect going on, you know? This whole lack of closure thing. But if you fuck her, you'll see that she's not some elusive goddess or whatever but just an ordinary woman."

Luke sat down on the bleacher seat and wiped his face with the hem of his tee shirt. "You're out of your mind. Even granting your premise, which I don't, how in the hell am I going to fuck Caroline Jones? She's living in New York City, and—"

Too late, he realized his mistake.

Joe grinned. "How do you know where she's living?"

Because he'd kept track of her, that's how. He knew when she graduated from college. He knew when she started going by Kali instead of Caroline. He knew when she produced her first play, and when she got her first TV job. He'd seen *Negative Space*, the little independent film she'd written and directed. He'd watched *Roommates* on TV, and tried to identify which scenes and lines were hers.

He avoided Joe's question. "Even if she lived right next door, how would I convince her to sleep with me? We didn't exactly part on good terms, in case you've forgotten. Unless I tie her down and force her, I don't think she'd ever—"

He stopped suddenly, his brain temporarily shut down by a vision of Caroline . . . Kali . . . naked and tied to his bed, her slim legs spread wide and her long dark hair fanned out on his pillow.

The image made him a little light-headed.

Joe shook his head impatiently. "You're Luke fucking Tanner, for Christ's sake. You're not some kid from the wrong side of the tracks anymore. When's the last time you had trouble talking a woman into your bed?"

Senior year of high school.

Shit. What if Joe was right?

He still felt guilty for breaking up with Maria. When she'd asked him what had gone wrong, he hadn't had an answer for her.

Because nothing had gone wrong. Maria was perfect, and any guy would be lucky to have her. The tabloids had all declared that she was The One, and there'd been wide-spread speculation that he'd be popping the question any day.

Instead, he'd broken up with her.

All he'd ever wanted was to be free of his past. If there was any chance that Joe was right, that Caroline Jones was still in his head somehow, didn't he owe it to himself to exorcise this one last ghost?

He probably wouldn't be able to fuck her, but he could see her. Maybe that would be enough to get closure, or whatever the hell he needed. To break whatever spell she might still be casting over him.

And so a plan was born. He did a little research, and found out that Kali was working on a brand new show. It was her baby—she was the creator, writer, and director.

In an interview she'd done for one of the trade magazines, she'd talked about her plan to cast unknown actors—fresh faces that the audience could connect with on their own terms, without any associations from past roles.

A big smile crossed his face when he read that particular tidbit. The last thing Kali would want was a big name actor interested in her little drama—especially him.

On the other hand, he'd worked with enough movie and network executives to know that they wouldn't feel the same way. If Luke Tanner expressed interest in *Ghosts*—including the willingness to work for what they could pay him—there was no way they'd ever turn him down.

And that would make Kali absolutely insane.

It would take a saint to resist the opportunity to get revenge for past humiliation, and Luke was no saint. He picked up the phone to call his agent and get the ball rolling.

Of course he had no desire to commit himself to a TV show, but he wouldn't need to. All he had to do was show up in New York, wreak a little well-deserved havoc in Kali's life, and leave—spell broken and closure achieved.

It was the perfect plan.

Or at least, it was the perfect plan until she'd barreled into him in the hallway, and he'd grabbed her arms to keep her from falling.

The first thing he noticed was that she smelled exactly the same—like clean laundry that's been hung out in the sun to dry, so that all you wanted to do was bury your face in it and breathe. It was that scent that made him hang onto her, out of sheer instinct, even after she started to pull away.

After that, he noticed other things. Her silky brown hair was cut short, and even though he felt a brief pang of loss for the long tresses he'd once adored, he had to acknowledge that the new look suited her. With her big eyes and dark brows, she looked like Audrey Hepburn in *Roman Holiday*.

She was wearing glasses now, which gave her already serious face an almost severe look. He was willing to bet she wore them for that reason, convinced that it would make people take her more seriously . . . or keep them at a distance.

She still dressed conservatively—boring as shit, in other words—and wore hardly any makeup.

But those were just details. His first sight of her hit him like a punch in the gut, with the same impact he'd felt so many years ago. And in that moment, he knew that Joe had been right. He had to shake loose of whatever hold she still had on him.

She obviously resented his presence here with every fiber of her being. It gave him some satisfaction to know he could still affect her, even if it was only negative. It was also obvious that no one she worked with knew that they'd gone to high school together, which made him wonder what else she was keeping to herself.

"They don't know who you are, do they?" he asked softly as they stood in front of the elevators.

Her head whipped around. "I don't know what you mean," she said tightly, just as the elevator doors slid open.

There wasn't anyone else in here, which meant they'd have a few moments alone—especially if he stopped the elevator between floors, which he did.

"What the hell are you doing?"

She stretched out a hand for the control panel, but he grabbed her wrist before she reached it.

It was the first time he'd touched her bare skin. For a split second, both of them froze. Sensation radiated through his body from that single point of contact, and he had to fight the sudden urge to pull her closer.

Then she jerked away and went for the panel on the other side of the doors.

"Just give me one minute, Kali."

Her hand stopped just before she touched the panel. After a moment she let it drop, but she kept her back to him.

He had a perfect view of the nape of her neck, which was almost unbearably tempting.

"Why are you here, Luke?" she asked, her voice wary. "What do you want from me?"

"Maybe I just want to see you again."

Her shoulders stiffened. "If that's really all you wanted, you could have Skyped me or something."

"If I had Skyped you, would you have answered?"

A short silence. "That's not the point. The point is—"

"Would you mind turning around? I'm having a hard time connecting with the back of your neck."

Actually, he had no problem at all with the back of her neck. He'd like to devote hours to the back of her neck. But he was feeling oddly desperate to look into her eyes again.

She gave a heavy sigh as she turned, folding her arms and glaring at him.

Her short hair framed her face perfectly, highlighting her high, wide cheekbones and full mouth. Even with her jaw tense and her brows drawn together in a frown, she was still the loveliest woman he'd ever seen.

"What you're doing is *unconscionable*."

He leaned against the wall of the elevator and grinned at her. "Yeah? And what is it you think I'm doing?"

"You know perfectly well. Pretending to be interested in *Ghosts*. Getting Tom excited for nothing. He thinks you're going to save his job, did you know that? The network's ready to let him go, and then you come along like some *deus ex machina*, the wonderful miracle that's going to save his job and my show."

He zeroed in on her last comment. "Is your show in trouble, then?"

She pressed her lips together, and he could tell she hadn't meant to let that slip.

He'd let that one go for now. "I'm sorry about Tom," he said instead. "I hope he doesn't lose his job."

"Like you care," she snapped.

He raised an eyebrow. "How do you know I don't?"

"Because you and I both know why you're really here."

"And why's that?"

"To get back at me."

It took an effort to keep from smiling in satisfaction. "Yeah? Get back at you for what?"

Too late, she realized her mistake. Now she'd have to talk about what she'd done. Out loud. To him.

She did her best to sidestep. "You know what I'm talking about. For . . . for how things ended between us in high school."

No way was he letting her off the hook that easily.

"Refresh my memory, Caroline. How did things end between us?"

Her jaw tightened. "I go by Kali now."

He nodded. "Yeah, I know. The Hindu goddess of destruction. Very appropriate."

She glared at him. "She also represents creativity and female power."

"And female sexuality," he added.

She blushed so intensely that he could actually see the color rise in her cheeks. He stared, fascinated. All these years after high school, could she still be that shy about sex?

Her eyes slid away from his, and then she reached for the control panel and started the elevator again.

"Your minute's up," she said tersely, not looking at him.

"Everyone here knows you as Kali. I bet that means they don't know who your father is. Do they?"

She stared straight ahead, her eyes fixed on the elevator doors. "Since my father isn't a part of my life anymore, I've never felt a need to talk about him with my coworkers."

The big shot director wasn't in her life anymore? That was a surprise. Still . . .

"I'm sure he played his part, though."

"Played his part in what?" she asked suspiciously.

"In your current job. You can't tell me you got a gig like this without dropping a name or two along the way."

She jerked her head around to look at him, and then checked the floor display to see that they were between the third and fourth floors before she reached out to stop the elevator.

In the next instant she was facing him down, stabbing a forefinger towards his chest. "I didn't name drop to get where I am. That's why no one here knows who my father is. Because I didn't want to be accused of using connections to get ahead."

Man, she was pissed. Her cheeks were flushed, her eyes narrowed into slits, and all he could think about was hauling her against his body and kissing that soft, sweet mouth—in spite of the fact that all Kali wanted to do with her mouth was spit fire at him.

He was hard for her. Christ, he was hard for her. His one rational thought was that he couldn't let her see the power she still had over him. No, not him: his cock. His cock had always had a mind of its own when it came to this woman.

So he reached out to restart the elevator and said something calculated to drive her—or any self-respecting woman—insane.

"You're cute when you're angry."

The elevator doors opened, and he stepped out into the lobby with a feeling of relief. But the relief was short-lived, as he turned to see her coming out of the elevator after him. In the sunlight that spilled in through the lobby windows she was even more beautiful, her skin glowing and her eyes snapping, and every inch of her crackling with life.

"You arrogant piece of—" She stopped suddenly, realizing that they were once again in a public place.

He smiled down at her. "Yes? You were saying?"

Her chest rose as she took a deep breath, and his eyes dropped to her breasts. What was she wearing under her boring outfit? Boring underwear to match? Or did she secretly indulge in red lace and thongs?

"Look," she said, her voice cool in spite of a slight tremor. "If your goal was to come out here and rattle my cage, you can consider your mission accomplished. So you can go back to L.A. now."

The funny thing was, that *had* been his goal. Up until he'd seen her, all he'd wanted was to rattle her cage and get a little closure.

And now?

Now, his mind and motives were in turmoil. He wasn't sure what he wanted from Kali Jones anymore.

But he knew he hadn't gotten it yet.

"Have a good weekend, Kali," he said, before walking away in long, easy strides. All around him, people stopped what they were doing to watch him pass. He wondered for a moment if Kali was watching, too, but he didn't turn to find out.

CHAPTER 3

Have a good weekend, Kali.

No hint in those words as to his next move. But she had to believe that whatever entertainment value she possessed wouldn't be enough to keep him in New York for long. His life and career were in Hollywood, and sticking around to torture her would have to have a diminishing appeal.

"Here's your keycard, Ms. Jones. You're in room 515," the man behind the desk told her.

She smiled her thanks and headed for the elevators.

Here, at least, she wouldn't have to worry about seeing Luke Tanner. For the next few days she could concentrate on work and the beautiful scenery surrounding this upstate resort. This would be a chance to regroup professionally and emotionally, a chance to figure out a way to save her show and Tom's job without Luke, a chance to—

Halfway across the lobby, she froze. There was a commotion at the entrance, and a ripple of excitement among the hotel staff.

Slowly, very slowly, she turned to follow the direction of all the eyes.

Luke Tanner was coming through the door, surrounded by a fluttering crowd of hotel employees and guests.

He glanced casually around the elegant lobby, and when his eyes met hers he smiled. Then he waved.

The gaggle of fans around him turned to see who he'd waved to, but Kali was already gone. She practically ran for the elevators, and she breathed a sigh of relief when she found one waiting. Once inside she stabbed repeatedly at the button for the fifth floor, keeping her eyes down until the doors closed with a glacial slowness whose sole purpose seemed to be to make her heart pound so hard it hurt a little.

Oh, God.

"What is Luke Tanner doing here?" she asked Tom twenty minutes later. They had adjoining rooms, and she'd knocked on his door after unpacking her things with hands that refused to stop trembling.

Tom shrugged. "He called one of the network bigwigs, told them how excited he was to be talking to us about the show, and got himself invited along for the weekend." He led the way out to his balcony, gesturing towards one of the lounge chairs and settling down in the other. "Diane let me know on the way up this morning. Apparently Luke also told them that the network was lucky to have the two of us on their team, and that the prospect of working with us was what sparked his interest in *Ghosts*. Of course you're the one he really wants to work with, but I'm pretty chuffed that he mentioned me, too. It definitely scored me some points with Diane," he added with satisfaction.

"You're a wonderful producer, Tom. You shouldn't need Luke Tanner to remind the network of that fact."

But as she stared out over the crystal blue lake and the rise of the Adirondacks beyond, she acknowledged, grudgingly, that it was a nice thing for Luke to have done. Of course when they failed to get Luke's signature on a contract it could all fall apart, but . . .

"What are you wearing to the dinner tonight?" Tom asked. He loved fashion, and her total lack of interest in clothes was a never-ending source of pain for him.

She shrugged. "I brought a couple of dresses. Both black. One of them even has some sequins on it. Happy?"

"Black with sequins. Not that one you bought last year for the Emmys? Please tell me it's something new."

"Well, no. It's the same one. But this isn't an awards ceremony or anything, just a dinner."

"A formal dinner with the network executives—and Luke Tanner."

She bristled a little. "I'm not going to dress up for Luke. Especially since every other woman there will. He doesn't need any more sops to his ego, believe me."

Tom sighed. "We need to be at our best this weekend. You and I both know that Luke might not do the show, so we need to leverage his interest and our visibility while we can."

She stared at him. "That's remarkably pragmatic of you, Tom. What happened to your wide-eyed optimism?"

He grinned at her. "It's still there. In fact, it's telling me that tonight, for once, you'll let me choose your outfit."

"Tom—"

"I spotted something at the resort boutique that would be perfect for you."

"Tom—"

"Pretty please with sugar on top?"

She sighed. "Fine."

"I'm really glad you said that, because I already bought the dress." He reached for a shopping bag on the other side of his chair and handed it to her. "Consider it an early Christmas present." He checked his watch. "You'd better go or you'll be late for your appointment."

"What appointment?"

"At the spa downstairs. Hair and makeup and a mani-pedi. Enjoy."

"Tom—"

"See you at dinner, sweetie."

Two hours later she was looking at herself in the bathroom mirror, wondering if she still had time to change.

It wasn't that the dress Tom had picked out was bad. It was good, in fact. Beautiful, even. But what if Luke thought she'd worn it for him?

She wriggled her shoulders to confirm that the silk chiffon top wouldn't slip and reveal any more cleavage than it already did. The cap sleeves seemed secure, but the light material and low-cut bodice made her feel half-naked.

Okay, that decided it. The black dress might be boring, but it didn't make her self-conscious. She was going to change.

She started to unzip and then stopped, struck once more by how beautiful the colors were. The dress was like a Monet painting come to life, a shifting wash of moss green and sapphire and indigo and violet. The colors made her want to wear it, even though the material clung to her upper body and the light, floating skirt barely came to her knees. It wasn't risqué, exactly . . . just sexy.

And Kali Jones didn't do sexy.

But as she stood staring at herself, uncertain, there was a knock on the door.

Okay, *that* decided it. Tom was here to walk downstairs with her, and she shouldn't keep him waiting. Plus, he'd be disappointed if she didn't wear the dress.

Except that it wasn't Tom standing there when she pulled open her door. It was Luke Tanner, looking like every woman's fantasy in black dress pants and a navy blue silk shirt, a hint of stubble on his jaw and a half smile on his face.

Her greeting to Tom froze on her lips.

But for once, Luke seemed more rattled than she did. His eyes slid down her body and back up to her face, and he spoke one word into the electric silence.

"Jesus."

Luke's reaction shouldn't matter to her, but it did. In spite of herself, a flush of pleasure warmed her skin.

"What are you doing here?" she asked, when she finally trusted herself to speak.

"I—" his voice came out a little husky, and he paused to clear his throat. "I ran into Tom. He said he was going to walk you down to dinner, and I asked if I could, instead."

His gaze slid down to her cleavage before jerking back up again. "This doesn't seem like your usual, uh, style."

She shifted her weight. "Tom picked the dress out," she said, irked when she heard the defensiveness in her voice.

Luke smiled a little. "He did, huh? No wonder you trust him to produce your shows."

His blue eyes were warm, and for once his smile seemed friendly and not mocking. He seemed less like a movie star and more like the Luke Tanner she'd known so many years ago.

In this mood, maybe she could talk to him. Reason with him.

She took a deep breath. "Luke. I don't know why you came here, but please, please, go back home to L.A.. I can't believe you really want to hurt me after all these years. That was all so long ago, and . . . I'm sorry."

Instead of softening him, her appeal made his eyes harden. "Sorry for what?"

He'd done that yesterday, too—challenged her to talk about their past.

Well, could she? If that's what it took to send him out of her life?

Her stomach tightened at the sudden swirl of remembered emotion—guilt, shame, grief, anger. All part of the hard knot of misery she'd buried deep, never to be revisited.

The silence went on for a long time. After a minute, she realized her hands were clenched into fists. She made a conscious effort to relax them but tension still reverberated throughout her body.

"Kali," Luke said after another minute, and she looked up at him. His expression was neutral, his eyes opaque. "I've got a proposition for you," he went on, and her breath hitched in her chest.

"What is it?" she asked, her voice guarded.

"Do you remember that night at Joe's house? The night we played truth or dare?"

Of course she remembered. How could she forget? It was after graduation and weeks after their disastrous prom night. She hadn't wanted to go to the party, knowing that Luke might be there, but her dad told her he was sick of her 'living like a nun' and had insisted she go.

They'd played all kinds of silly high school games that night, in a rush of nostalgia, maybe, for the life they were leaving behind. She'd stayed out of most of them, standing in the shadows by the bookcases in Joe's living room. But when they'd started truth or dare after finishing spin the bottle, Luke had looked right at her.

"Truth or dare?" he'd asked, his voice cold and hard.

"Truth," she'd answered, terrified of what he might dare her do.

He'd gotten up from the couch and gone over to her. "Why did you stand me up on prom night?"

She'd stared at him for about five seconds before turning and running blindly out of the house.

Until yesterday afternoon, that was the last time she'd seen Luke Tanner.

She smoothed her hands over the material of her skirt. "I remember," she said gruffly. "What about it?"

"Let's have a game this weekend for old times' sake. If you'll agree to that, I'll leave for L.A. on Monday morning. And you'll never have to see me again."

She sank her teeth into her lower lip as she pondered. Was this as straightforward as it seemed?

"How many rounds?" she asked, finally.

"Two."

"If I agree . . . will you tell the network people it's not my fault or Tom's that you're not doing the show? And that you still hope to work with us sometime in the future?"

"Sure."

"But you won't. I mean, I want the execs to think you might, but I don't want to actually work with you."

"I get it, Kali."

"Then . . . okay."

He slid his hands into his pockets and leaned against the doorframe. "Truth or dare?"

"Dare."

* * *

Luke's eyebrows lifted in surprise. He hadn't been expecting that. He'd thought the game would be a way to navigate the tension between them, to finally get an answer to the question that had eaten at him for ten years.

He wasn't quite sure what to do next, and he could see from the satisfied gleam in Kali's eyes that she knew it. He'd come to New York to mess with her head, and she always seemed to end up messing with his.

God, she looked fucking incredible tonight. He hadn't been expecting that, either. But when she'd opened her door he'd almost passed out.

She was wearing a floating cloud of nothing much, a delicate watercolor of a dress that made her skin look like alabaster. He was willing to bet Tom had picked out her shoes, too, since Kali never wore high heels. Her legs were bare and shapely and the neckline of that dress ended in a point just above her belly button, giving him a mouthwatering glimpse of skin that seldom saw the light of day—the skin on the inside of her perfect breasts, softer than the softest silk.

She wore a blue headband in her short hair, holding the waves away from her face. Her makeup, for once, had been beautifully applied. Even her glasses seemed like the perfect touch—a visible signifier of the bookish, hopelessly nerdy personality he'd once fallen in love with.

Once but never again, he thought with an odd twinge of panic. He'd come out to the east coast to lay his old ghosts to rest, not to make the same mistake twice.

"So what's my dare?" she asked carelessly, obviously relishing the fact that he was momentarily at a loss.

"I'm not sure yet," he said, keeping his voice as careless as hers. "I'll have to think it over."

She shrugged. "Well, you can't take too long. I don't want you dragging this out. I'll give you until midnight tonight."

"Fine."

"Fine."

There was a pause while Luke tried to remember what the hell he was doing here in the first place.

"We should probably head down now," she said after a moment. "The dinner's starting at eight."

"Right."

The quiet elegance of the resort's private dining room was the perfect backdrop for Kali tonight, with her sylph-like dress and her delicate loveliness. He was sure that every man in the room must be staring at her, but when he took a look around, he saw that masculine interest was focused on the gorgeous redhead who starred in *Roommates*.

She was stunning, no question. But as far as he was concerned, she couldn't hold a candle to Kali Jones.

She didn't radiate the prickly, restless intelligence that Kali did. She didn't have Kali's elfin grace. And she didn't have the eager, contagious passion that Kali had when she was talking about something she cared about—like right now, as she answered a network VP's question about *Ghosts.*

This dining room had been reserved for the network people, and he and Kali had been seated at a back table by the far wall. Kali sat at the end and Luke was on her right, with a perfect view of her as she spoke to the man on her other side.

She used her hands to illustrate points, as though words weren't enough. She was so charming, so compelling . . . he didn't understand how any man in the room could keep his eyes off her. The woman next to him was chattering away about something—his last movie, he thought—but all he needed to do to maintain the conversation was nod his head once in a while. That left him free to watch Kali . . . and to remember the first time they met.

It was the summer before freshman year, at a theater arts camp in L.A.. Kali was there as a member of the Hollywood elite—the daughter of actress Meredith Michaels and her equally famous husband, director Henry Jones. Luke was there on scholarship.

He hung around with the cool kids, both rich and poor, while Kali stayed by herself most of the time. At one of those let's-get-to-know-each-other campfire things, she revealed that she was homeschooled, which helped explain her total lack of social skills.

He'd dismissed her in his mind as a solitary weirdo, and was already waiting to hear from the next person in the circle—a gorgeous blonde girl—when she answered the question about her favorite movies and TV shows. "*Buffy the Vampire Slayer, Freaks and Geeks, Chasing Amy, Edward Scissorhands,* and *Dazed and Confused.*"

He stared at her. The girls so far had given completely predictable answers—*Titanic* and *Braveheart* and *Dawson's Creek*. The girl next to her went with those, adding *Casablanca* to the list to show off her classic movie chops. But Luke barely glanced at her. He was staring at the pixie-faced girl with the long dark hair who had already withdrawn back into her own private world, gazing off into space and talking to herself like the solitary weirdo she was.

The next morning, he got up early to go for a swim. Kali was there before him, doing some strange kind of undulating stroke. When she caught sight of him she swam immediately for the side of the pool and got out, grabbing her towel without looking at him and drying herself off in a hurry.

"What were you doing?" he asked, walking around the pool to meet her. "What kind of stroke was that?"

She pulled on her tee shirt and shorts over her bathing suit before answering him. She had a pixie body to go with her pixie face—small breasts, a tiny waist, and slender hips. Cute but not spectacular.

"Oh, it's just this stupid thing I do," she said dismissively, starting to walk past him without meeting his eyes.

"What stupid thing? Tell me."

She stopped, shrugging her shoulders. "I pretend I'm a mermaid," she said, clutching at the damp towel around her neck.

He laughed, but not in a mean way, and after a moment she started to smile. "I know it's dumb," she said shyly.

"No, it's cute. I bet you used to do that horse thing, too," he said, noticing for the first time how big her eyes were.

"What horse thing?"

"You know. That thing girls do, where your lower body is the galloping horse and your upper body is the rider."

Now they laughed together. "Yeah, I did," she admitted. "When I was, like, six."

"You wrote that play about the mermaid, didn't you?" he asked suddenly. The kids who were in the writing program submitted their work to the kids in the acting and directing programs, and her play had been a hundred times better than anything else they'd read so far. "The one about the teenage boy who goes to the ocean and meets a mermaid."

She nodded, her cheeks pink.

"It's one of the ones we picked to produce. I'm going to audition for the lead."

Her big eyes got even bigger. "You are?"

"Yeah."

From that point on, they'd been friends. He didn't make a move on her—at fourteen, he'd still been focused on blonde hair and big boobs as his criteria for that kind of interest—but he liked her more than anyone else at camp. They talked for hours about books and music and movies, and their hopes and dreams for the future. She knew he was poor and he knew she was rich, but for that one golden summer it didn't seem to matter.

When camp ended, she went back to homeschooling and he went to high school—a private academy he'd gotten into on a full academic scholarship. They emailed each other a few times freshman year but he'd gotten busy fast, with schoolwork and his first real girlfriend. He also had to deal with the rich assholes who took every opportunity to tear him down, and a father who drank and lost jobs and told his son he'd never amount to anything. Within a few months, he'd stopped emailing the odd, interesting girl he'd met at camp.

And then, senior year, she started going to his school. Her parents had divorced that summer and her mother had gone into a treatment facility for mental illness. She'd been the one who'd insisted on homeschooling her only child, and once she was out of the picture her father decided it was high time his backward daughter got a taste of 'normal' life.

Luke was a lot smarter at eighteen than he'd been at fourteen, and when he saw Kali again he recognized his feelings for what they were: lust and longing in equal measure. She was just as odd, just as interesting, and just as smart as she'd been four years ago, but this time, something about her elfin face and small, slender body turned his crank like it had never been turned before.

Ten years hadn't changed that. Kali still turned him on more than any woman he'd ever met. She was leaning forward now, her eyes alight, completely caught up in what she was saying.

There was a sudden, sharp ache in his sternum. The two of them used to talk like that, for the few short, blissful months during senior year when they'd been friends.

"I've always been fascinated by the idea of ghosts. They can represent so many things, you know? Memory, regret, life and death, immortality. You've seen *A Christmas Carol*, right? One of my favorite scenes is when Marley's ghost is talking to Scrooge and he looks outside to see a homeless woman with a baby. And he's in agony because he can't do anything to help her. A reminder that people need to live fully in the moment, to help each other while they're able. Ghosts remind us of eternity and also the transience of life. That's the tragedy and beauty of being human—we're finite but we touch the infinite, and we're not completely at home in either reality. Do you know what I mean?"

She wasn't talking to him, but he heard himself say "Yes," even as the VP said "I think so," a little cautiously, before he shook his head and smiled. "You creative types," he said jovially. "You're too deep for me. I guess we're all good at different things, right?" He checked his watch and rose from his seat. "Time for my little speech," he said, moving to the podium that had been set up in the front of the room.

"I did it again," Kali muttered, taking a gulp of wine. They'd finished dinner, but Kali had only had a few bites of food along with two glasses of wine.

"Did what?" Luke asked.

She glanced up at him. She'd hardly spoken to him during the meal, and he knew the only reason she was speaking to him now was because of the alcohol buzzing in her veins.

"I talk too much. You heard what he said, didn't you? That I'm 'too deep'. That's code for boring. The execs think I'm too intellectual, and that it's going to show in my scripts. Which it never does, by the way. My first priority is always telling a good story. My ideas are just there in the subtext, to make the story richer." She sighed. "But I should know by now not to share the stuff in my head with the network people. I always end up feeling like the nerdy kid no one wants to talk to, and they never get what I'm saying."

He couldn't help smiling. "You worried about this same thing in high school."

She frowned at him. "What do you mean?"

"You'd go for days without saying anything in class, and then you wouldn't be able to stand it anymore and you'd talk, and you'd always say something interesting and original. But after class you'd be embarrassed because you actually expressed yourself out loud and everyone must be thinking what a dork you were, and you'd swear you'd never, ever do it again. You said writing was much better than talking, just like art was better than life. And then you'd last about a week before the words inside you would explode and you'd talk in class and start the whole process over again."

She smiled a little. "I did that?"

He'd forgotten what it felt like to have Kali smile at him. "Yeah. But you didn't have anything to worry about then, and you don't have anything to worry about now. Don't you know that smart is sexy?"

They looked at each other for a moment. Then Kali's gaze dropped to her wine glass, and she ran a finger over the rim. "Maybe you thought so once. But it's pretty obvious that your interests have changed since high school."

He frowned. "What's that supposed to mean?"

"Come on, Luke. I've seen the movies you've made over the last few years. You're not exactly doing Shakespeare."

He ignored the veiled insult and zeroed in on something else. "You've seen my movies?"

She shrugged. "Well, sure. The whole world has. You make blockbusters, remember?"

"Is that the only reason you've seen them?"

"Yes."

The VP started his speech, and people angled their chairs towards the front of the room as the lights dimmed. He welcomed everyone to the network's annual retreat and hoped that they'd enjoyed their dinner. It was now his pleasure to give the weekend's keynote address, and he wanted to start with a little anecdote from his recent trip to Europe . . .

They were sitting at the back of the room, and Kali had a wall behind her. With everyone facing away the space between them seemed more intimate, almost private. Luke tuned out the VP and moved his chair closer to Kali's.

"I think you're lying," he said softly. "I think you watched those movies because I was in them. I think you went home afterwards and fantasized about me."

He only meant to tease her, to knock her off balance a little. But when her gaze jerked up to meet his and her cheeks flooded with color, he wondered suddenly if what he'd said might actually be true.

Her expression turned fierce as she hitched her chair closer to his. "Let me make this perfectly clear. I don't have a secret crush on you, Luke. I don't think you're sexy, I don't think you're charming, and I don't fantasize about you. Ever. I think you're an arrogant jerk who got bored one day and decided to mess with my life, and all I want is to send you back to L.A. where you belong. So if you don't mind, give me a dare so we can get this stupid game started."

He was a hundred percent sure it wasn't her intention, but when Kali got that look in her eyes it made him hard as a rock. His heart beat faster, and the hunger to be inside her took over his body. He had to clench his fists to keep from throwing her over his shoulder and carrying her off to his cave.

Except for one explosive kiss the day he'd asked her to the prom, he hadn't touched her back in high school. She'd been so innocent . . . because of her overprotective mother, she'd never even been on a date. He, on the other hand, had slept with a dozen girls, all of them as experienced as he was.

Kali's innocence had been oddly intimidating, as though contact with him might sully her somehow. For months he'd resisted his desire for her and tried to be satisfied with friendship, since he knew she wasn't ready for more.

It had almost killed him. Just like sitting beside her was killing him now.

But he wasn't a kid anymore, and neither was she.

He took a deep breath. "I dare you to sit without moving or speaking for ten minutes."

She sat back in surprise. "That's it?" She thought about it for a moment. "I suppose that's your snide way of telling me I do talk too much. Well, fine."

She grabbed her purse and pulled her cell phone out of it. After a puzzled moment he realized she was programming her alarm to ring after ten minutes, and in spite of the tension vibrating through him, he had to smile. She'd give him ten minutes to the second and no more.

It would be enough.

She set the phone on the table and turned her eyes back to the front of the room, her arms folded across her chest and a sour expression on her face.

They'd moved their chairs closer to each other over the last few minutes, and her right leg was only inches away. The thought of her soft, bare skin made his palms tingle, and the anticipation was so sweet that he made himself wait a few extra seconds, just to prove to himself that he could.

Then, under the cover of the tablecloth, he put his hand on her thigh.

CHAPTER 4

Kali jerked her leg away in outrage, only just stopping herself from saying something out loud.

But she managed to stay silent. Did he think he could win the game that easily? Well, he could forget it. She was made of tougher stuff than Luke Tanner realized. She wasn't an innocent schoolgirl now, who could be overwhelmed by a simple touch.

Luke's eyes, like hers, had been trained on the speaker. Now he turned his head to look at her, and something in his intense, predatory gaze made her go still, as if she were a mouse in the shadow of a hawk's wings.

He didn't say a word, but his eyes stayed on hers as he found her leg again.

The big hand circling her thigh was blatantly possessive. When she tried to pull away again he gripped her harder, tighter.

And then, finally, she understood.

This was the dare. She had to sit here for ten minutes while he . . . what? Exactly how far was he planning to take this?

She stared at him, her expression stony, and he looked back at her. He seemed cool and detached, his blue eyes giving nothing away. His face had never looked more handsome or more remote.

Then his fingers moved, softly, massaging the muscles just above her knee.

And one corner of his mouth rose half an inch.

He was taunting her. He didn't think she would last ten minutes. He thought she'd give up without a fight.

And suddenly, the only thing that mattered was proving him wrong. Proving that his touch wouldn't affect her in the least. That his vaunted sexual power could work on every woman in the world except for her.

So she gave an impatient sigh, as though she were bored. Then she settled back in her chair with her eyes once again fixed on the network VP, who was droning on now about social media and viral marketing and God knew what else.

She felt Luke's gaze on her for a moment longer. Then, out of the corner of her eye, she watched him turn his head to face the speaker again. She breathed a quick sigh of relief and tried to ignore the waves of pleasure that had begun to radiate from his palm on her bare skin.

Her relief was soon over. Because now his hand slipped under her dress and started to move slowly up her thigh.

She stopped breathing. Another few inches and he'd be touching the edge of her underwear.

She could handle it. She could. This was nothing but a stupid, childish game.

Except that there was nothing childish about the way Luke made her feel. There never had been. Long before she could put a name to the feelings he aroused in her, she'd known that they belonged to the woman she was becoming and not the girl she had been.

When she was fourteen, her longing for Luke had been so unfamiliar, so new and strange and terrifying, that she'd pushed it aside and refused to think about it. When she met him again at eighteen, it was still terrifying . . . but she hadn't been able to push it aside. Her feelings for him had grown until he was all she could think about, but she couldn't imagine ever crossing the line of friendship to act on her attraction.

It was too enormous a thing to contemplate. She had been so sheltered by her mother . . . she would never be on an equal footing with the other girls in his life. She could never think of Luke the way they did. The chasm between her innocence and his experience was too wide. All she'd wanted was to love him silently and desperately, from afar.

She'd been afraid of physical passion, and because of that she'd always been a little afraid of Luke. He was so big and male and sexual—and she hadn't been ready to deal with any of that. That fateful day when he'd kissed her after school and asked her to the prom, she'd known she was out of her depth.

And now?

Luke's hand ghosted over those last few inches, and he began to trace the edge of her panties with his fingertips.

She couldn't believe this was happening. She was sitting in a dining room filled with a hundred colleagues, and Luke Tanner was slipping a finger under the elastic to stroke the sensitive crease on the inside of her thigh.

She risked a glance at him, but he wasn't looking her way. His face was in profile to her and his gaze was fixed on the VP as though he were making the most fascinating speech Luke had ever heard. There was no hint in his expression or in his body language that he had his hand on her, stroking her, making her skin tingle with sweet, shocked awareness.

She was sure he wouldn't go any further than this. Her conviction was confirmed a few moments later, when his fingers retreated from under the edge of her panties.

She felt a rush of relief . . . and a twinge of regret. What Luke had done was mortifying and inappropriate, but it was also incredibly arousing, and a thread of forbidden excitement had been woven into her embarrassment.

Then she bit back a gasp as Luke covered her mound with his big, warm palm.

In the years since high school, she'd had three lovers. But no man had ever touched her like this, so firmly and possessively, as though all her secret places belonged to him.

Her body started to quiver.

And then he was massaging her through the thin material of her panties, his hand so large he seemed to touch her everywhere at once.

It was too much. She was pierced by sensation, overwhelmed by it. She needed to move, to wriggle, to squirm.

But she didn't. She wouldn't. She was going to beat Luke's dare if it killed her, and—

She froze. Luke's hand slid up to her belly and then down, down inside her panties, his fingers spreading her wide as his palm brushed over her clit, and even though she held back her gasp she couldn't hold back the rush of moisture that was her body's answer to his touch.

He went still.

He knew, now. He knew she liked what he was doing . . . or that parts of her did. Would he turn and look at her with that glint in his eyes? Smile at her in triumph?

She held her breath, waiting. But he kept his head turned away, his eyes still fixed on the front of the room, his expression cool and detached and even stern.

He wasn't laughing at her. And then his hand began to move, exploring her slowly, softly, his fingers gliding gently over her most delicate skin and making her tingle, not just where he was touching her but everywhere.

A thousand pin pricks made her nipples harden and her toes curl.

His fingers delved deeper, almost penetrating her. And she wanted him to. She wanted those long fingers inside her.

Oh, God, she was so wet for him. She didn't think she'd ever been this wet for a man.

And then Luke gave the first sign that he wasn't made of stone. A harsh breath escaped him, and her gaze jerked to his face.

His eyes were still glued to the front of the room, but she saw the muscles of his throat move as he swallowed.

He was excited. Her response to his touch was exciting him.

She surrendered to her own arousal in a sudden melting rush. She closed her eyes and moved for the first time, spreading her legs a few inches wider. Luke gave another ragged, uneven breath, and then he thrust two fingers into her as deep as they would go.

She bit her lip to keep from moaning out loud. His fingers were moving in a deliberate, explicit rhythm. He was fucking her, pulling out and pushing back in, the heel of his hand bumping against her clit with every thrust and starting a slow burn that spread through her entire body.

She was awash in sensation. Her body felt heavy and weightless at the same time, languorous and voluptuous and vibrating with pleasure, her very fingertips pulsating with the slow beat of her blood.

More. She needed more. She moved against him instinctively, pressing into his hand. Luke stilled for a moment, and then he pulled his fingers out of her so he could concentrate on her clit, working her in ever tightening circles.

Oh, God—she was going to come.

She opened her eyes to scan the area around them, but the VP was still going strong and there wasn't a waiter or waitress in sight.

Her heart was thundering, her blood rushing in her veins. Her eyes closed again as her hands clamped around the table edge, holding on for dear life.

Was she really going to have an orgasm in public? Luke must have sold his soul to the devil in exchange for this kind of skill.

She was so close. Nothing could stop this from happening. Not an earthquake or a tidal wave or—

The tinny sound of The Ramones' *I Wanna Be Sedated* emanating from her cell phone.

Her eyes flew open. Under the table, Luke's hand went still.

A beat went by. The ringtone wasn't terribly loud, but a few people turned towards her, frowns of disapproval on their faces. She grabbed for the phone and turned it off, her face even redder than it must have been already.

Her heart was pounding, her body trembling. She ached for release so much it hurt.

She gripped the phone until her knuckles turned white. She couldn't meet Luke's eyes, even though she could feel him looking at her. His hand was still on her body. Finally, after what seemed like an eternity, he spoke.

"I can keep going," he said, his voice low and intimate.

She looked up then, and saw that his face was flushed, too. He was breathing unevenly, and his blue eyes were fixed on hers with an expression she couldn't read.

God, yes. *Please* yes.

Her mouth opened to say the words and then closed again. No matter how much she wanted to, she would not beg Luke Tanner to get her off.

Up until this point, everything that had happened between them was his idea. This was his game. He was the one who'd dared her to sit there, the one who'd put his hand on her. The fact that she'd enjoyed it didn't matter . . . unless she asked him to keep going. Then he'd have proof of his power over her. Proof that she wanted him.

On the other hand, if she walked away now, he didn't have proof of anything.

She cleared her throat. "I'm all set, thanks. If you wouldn't mind . . . ?" she glanced down at her lap and back up at him.

Slowly, as if he couldn't believe she was serious, he took his hand away from her body.

She grabbed her purse, stuffed her phone inside it, and rose shakily to her feet. "Please excuse me," she said primly, preparing to walk past him.

He rose to his feet and blocked her way, leaning down so he could whisper in her ear. "Going to the ladies' room to finish yourself off?" He shook his head. "It won't be the same."

The tickle of his breath made her shiver. "Don't flatter yourself," she hissed, stepping around him and walking away, holding her head high and praying she didn't look as flushed and disheveled as she felt.

She didn't go to the ladies' room. She went past the restrooms and into the lobby, and she didn't stop walking until she stepped into an elevator and pressed the button for her floor with a feeling of intense relief.

Damn Luke Tanner to hell, she thought a few minutes later, turning on the taps of her tub. Damn him in particular for making that crack about finishing herself off.

Because she really, really wanted to. And now she couldn't, because with that remark Luke had ensured that if she touched herself tonight she would think of him . . . and imagine that his hands were on her.

Oh, God, those hands.

She tried to forget about his hands as she sank into the bath. Unfortunately, the heat and the wetness and the fact that she was naked weren't the best deterrents to thinking about Luke.

She'd always known that he was capable of making a woman feel like that. There was an implicit promise in those intense blue eyes and that sexy half smile and those big, strong hands. She'd recognized that promise even at fourteen, before she'd known what to call it. And she'd always felt it. Every woman who looked at him felt it.

I think you watched those movies because I was in them. I think you went home afterwards and fantasized about me.

He'd hadn't meant it seriously, of course. He'd just been trying to jerk her chain. But the sad thing was, it was true. Luke Tanner had starred in her very first sexual fantasy, and even though she'd tried to replace him a thousand times since then, he was still her leading man in that particular capacity.

But not tonight, damn it. And not ever again. She was done thinking about Luke in any capacity whatsoever.

Two hours later, she had to acknowledge her utter failure in the don't-think-about-Luke department.

The last hour had been particularly miserable. She'd gone to bed early, hoping for the oblivion of sleep, and instead she'd tossed and turned. Despite her determination to think about anything except Luke, she had in fact thought about him until her body and mind were in such turmoil that she finally threw her pillow on the floor and got out of bed to pace.

Of course there was an easy solution to one part of her problem. Given how hot and bothered she was, she'd come apart in about five seconds if she touched herself.

But the specter of Luke Tanner would be hovering over her, even more than he was right now. Damn him and his stupid game and—

The game. Truth or dare. That's how all this had started, right? And they hadn't finished their first round.

It was her turn now. The ball was in her court.

She stopped pacing. An idea had come into her head that was as wickedly appealing as it was terrifying.

If she had the guts to do it then maybe, just maybe, she could finally turn the tables on Luke Tanner.

* * *

He was in hell.

His plan had backfired. He'd come here to let go of the past, to put Kali Jones behind him. But after feeling her come alive under his hands, feeling her respond to him and melt at his touch, all he wanted was to make her feel that way again. To get past her defenses and watch her come apart in his arms.

How the hell had she been able to walk away from that intensity? After she left he'd been disappointed, if not really surprised, when she didn't come back. God knew she'd run from him before. But she was an adult now, damn it. She ought to have the courage to face her own feelings, to—

There was a knock on his door. When he glanced at the clock, he saw it was after midnight.

Of course this wasn't the first time he'd had a late-night visitor in a hotel. If a woman was determined enough, she could get a man's room number.

And he thought he could guess who it was. After Kali had left the dining room, that redheaded actress had made a move on him. On another night she might have succeeded, but he'd let her down easy and headed back to his room, where he'd been pacing back and forth for the last hour.

Another knock, more impatient this time.

He sighed and went to the door, glancing through the peephole as he reached for the knob.

It wasn't the redhead. It was Kali.

He pulled the door open and stared at her. She looked back at him defiantly, as if they were in the middle of an argument. Her hair was tousled, her face was scrubbed clean of makeup, and she wasn't wearing her glasses. She was in sweatpants and an old Pretenders tee shirt, and her feet were bare.

A rush of desire hit him fast and hard.

He ordered himself to get a grip. She couldn't possibly be here for sex—not with that scowl on her face.

He opened his mouth to invite her in, but she spoke before he could.

"Truth or dare?" she asked belligerently.

"What?"

"The game. It's my turn. Truth or dare?"

Sweet holy heaven, maybe she *was* here for sex. Why else would she show up after midnight to play the game?

Please, God, let her be here for sex.

"Dare."

A spark of satisfaction lit her eyes. "I dare you to sit without moving or speaking for ten minutes."

Was she going to do to him what he'd done to her? He modified his prayer slightly. *Please, God, let her do to me what I did to her.*

"Where do you want me?" he asked huskily, not taking his eyes off her.

She glanced around the room for a moment. "There," she said, pointing to the armchair next to his bed.

She didn't say anything about taking his clothes off, so he left them on. He sensed that Kali wanted to be in charge and he was all for it. This was a side of her he'd never seen before, and he wanted to see a whole lot more.

He sank down into the chair and watched her come closer. Now that she'd made her first move he could see uncertainty in her eyes, warring with determination and other, hotter emotions.

His hands tightened on the arms of the chair. *Don't let her run away. Not this time.*

"When does my ten minutes start?" he asked.

He noticed suddenly that she wasn't wearing a bra under her tee shirt. And just like that, he went from hard to harder. He forced his hands to relax before he pulled out chunks of stuffing from the chair.

And damn if Kali didn't pull her cell phone from her pocket and program the alarm.

"It starts now," she said, setting the phone down on the bed.

She paused. Then, without looking at him, she shimmied out of her sweatpants, leaving them on the floor as she climbed onto the bed.

She wasn't wearing any underwear.

Sweet holy fuck.

A rush of pure adrenaline made his heart slam against his ribs. It was a miracle he managed to stay still, when every cell in his body was pulling him towards her.

She lay back against the pillows, still without looking at him. He watched her chest rise and fall as she took a deep breath. Then, very slowly, she opened her legs.

She wasn't going to do to him what he'd done to her. She was going to do . . . something else.

Christ, she was so beautiful. So fucking perfect. Those slender legs, firm and toned and sleek. And at the juncture of her thighs a triangle of softness, enticing and mesmerizing, a place he'd felt tonight but hadn't seen.

He wanted to see more. He wanted to see everything. And then, as if she'd read his mind, Kali slid both her hands down to frame her pussy, pausing for just a moment before she pressed her fingers into her outer folds and pulled them apart, revealing the silken, glistening, dusky pink skin inside.

The sight affected him like the scent of ripe peaches. His mouth started to water with the need to taste, to lick, to suck, to consume. He'd never wanted to own a woman's pussy the way he wanted to own Kali's.

Then she slid her fingers over that silky skin, tracing her folds softly, slowly. He felt heavy, drugged with lust, his nerve endings sending messages of pleasure to his brain. Her body opened further, revealing more secrets, and the honey of her arousal made her skin gleam like satin.

His hands twitched spasmodically. And then she settled two fingers over her clit and started to rub in lazy circles, spreading her legs even wider as she let her body arch back into the pillows.

Fuck.

His cock strained against his pants as she brought herself higher and higher. Her eyes were closed, her breath fast and shallow.

Was she imagining him right now? Picturing him thrusting into her?

And then her legs spasmed against the bed as she moaned and gasped, her skin flushing with hectic color.

As he watched her come down, slowly, he became aware that his body was as taut as a bowstring, his cock throbbing with the pulse that beat through his veins. His hands were clenched on the arms of his chair and his breath was coming in ragged pants.

After an endless minute, Kali closed her legs and sat up. She hadn't looked at him once this whole time. Now she met his eyes for the barest instant before looking down again, picking up her phone with a shaking hand.

"You have one more minute," she told him. She slid off the bed and pulled on her sweatpants, sliding her phone into her pocket before walking unsteadily towards his door.

She paused there for a moment, her back to him. Then she turned the knob, slipped out the door, and was gone.

CHAPTER 5

All the next day, Kali felt Luke's gaze on her. It was heavy and burning, like a brand.

Like a promise.

She'd woken up feeling the way you do after tying one on the night before. When you have to confront the fact that you behaved like a crazed, drunken fool.

Except that she hadn't been drunk.

Only crazy. And foolish.

What the hell had she been thinking? She hadn't turned the tables at all. She felt more vulnerable to Luke now, not less. She'd exposed herself to him—literally—and in the cold light of day she realized how easily he could use that against her.

She dreaded the first moment of seeing him again. The knowing look that would be in his eyes, the cocky grin that would make her shrivel up inside. Her heart tightened in her chest when she saw him downstairs at the breakfast buffet, surrounded by a small crowd of eager fans.

Last night's dinner had been in a private dining room, and the network people had treated Luke like a professional. There'd been no gushing, no autograph seeking, no requests for photos. This morning, though, he was at the mercy of his fame, and she watched out of the corner of her eye as he handled the situation, friendly with everyone as he loaded his plate and then excusing himself politely.

His eyes met hers as he emerged from the knot of people, and he stopped short. For a moment they stared at each other, and heat rose in her cheeks until she felt almost feverish.

She wasn't sure how long they might have stayed like that if Tom, who was sitting next to her, hadn't called out to Luke and waved him over.

Her gaze dropped to her plate as Luke took the chair across from hers, and she played with her food as he and Tom chatted about the merits of high protein diets. She had no reason to think he was looking at her, but somehow she knew that he was.

After a few minutes Tom started a conversation with someone at the next table, and she darted a glance at Luke.

Oh, God—he *was* looking at her.

She dropped her eyes immediately, but it was too late. She felt the weight of his gaze, fierce and intent, and darts of awareness made her stomach muscles tighten until she had to press a hand to her belly to calm herself down.

* * *

He sat in on her first meeting of the day, where she and other show creators were discussing their latest projects. She was so distracted by his presence, by the way the nape of her neck prickled when she felt his eyes on her, that she rattled through the first part of her presentation without really focusing on what she was saying.

" . . . and so one of the functions of the ghosts that haunt our main characters is to represent the choices they face. Past and present. Head and heart. Dreams and reality. But the ghosts aren't only foils for the living. I want them . . . some of them, anyway . . . to have real emotional arcs of their own. I want the show to touch on the spiritual aspect of ghosts—the question of the afterlife, and what it means to move on after death. I want there to be moments of real mystery, moments when the characters truly feel haunted. I want there to be a touch of the numinous, especially when we least expect it. I want there to be romance and sex and pathos. And of course, I want it to be funny," she added with a smile.

This drew a chuckle of appreciation from her colleagues. She had a reputation for being able to find the humor in any scene. According to company legend, the network CFO—who was widely believed never to have smiled at his own children—had actually laughed out loud during one of the episodes she'd written for *Roommates*.

Eric Felson, the guy she'd tapped to be her story editor, raised his hand. "It sounds like a fantastic show, Kali. I'm looking forward to working on it. I'm curious, though—you're targeting a wide audience, adults as well as teens. So why are three of your main characters high school students?"

She answered automatically, having addressed this question before.

"Adolescence is an intense time in our lives, a time that all adults can relate to. Emotions are powerful and dramatic, and our identities are shaped in ways it can be hard to escape later in life. Studies have shown that even decades later, people can still be defined by the way they saw themselves in high school . . . and by the way other people saw them. High school is the perfect setting for some of the themes we're exploring. The difficulty we face letting go of the past, and—"

She paused. As the words she'd just spoken echoed in her head she became intensely aware of Luke, who was sitting near the back of the room.

It took her a moment to recover the thread of what she was saying.

He didn't talk during the meeting, or afterwards, when everyone stood around chatting and waiting for lunch to begin. But Kali still felt his eyes on her, his gaze prickling her skin. She was filled with nervousness and a strange kind of exhilaration.

She tried to shake it off for the afternoon meetings, when individual shows had breakout sessions. Her first was with the team working on *Ghosts*, and when everyone was seated at the oblong table she felt relaxed and happy for the first time all day. She was excited to talk about their plans for the show.

Then Luke Tanner stuck his head in the room.

"Hey, everybody. Do you mind if I sit in?"

"Not at all." "Of course not!" "Come in!"

Kali grit her teeth as Luke took a seat, his posture easy and relaxed. She, on the other hand, was tight as a drum now that he was here, her heart beating uncomfortably fast.

Hannah Cole, her script supervisor, leaned across the table towards Luke. "I probably shouldn't ask this, but we're all a little curious. There've been rumors flying around that you're going to be joining our cast. I know I'm not the only one wondering if the rumors are true."

There was a murmur of assent around the table, and everyone turned eagerly to Luke, waiting to hear what he said. He glanced at her with one eyebrow raised, but she just shrugged her shoulders.

You're on your own, buddy.

Luke paused for a moment. "The truth is, I'm considering several different projects right now. I have to admit, though, that nothing can compare to *Ghosts* when it comes to creative storylines, rich characters, and original vision."

"But of course there are other factors to consider," Kali said drily. "Like money, for instance."

That earned her a few startled glances from some of the people in the room, but Luke just smiled. "Money's important, sure. But I have plenty of money at the moment. What I don't have are opportunities to work with a writing and directing team like this one. Of course," he went on, "I don't expect to be an automatic pick just because I'm a big name. In fact, I have it on good authority that you didn't want to work with well-known actors."

He grinned at her, looking suddenly boyish as a lock of dark blond hair fell across his forehead. Kali's nails dug into her palms as she felt an unexpected desire to brush it back.

"So I know I'll have to audition just like everybody else. In fact, I was wondering if I could have a mini-audition right now."

"What do you mean?" Hannah asked.

Luke reached for the inside pocket of his leather jacket and pulled out a sheaf of papers. "Kali handed out copies of her scripts this morning, and I had a chance to go through them at lunch. I was hoping I could read for the character I'm interested in."

"You mean Derek?" Kali asked. She'd been assuming all along that that was the character Luke wanted to play—or was pretending to want to play.

Derek Knight was a twenty-seven-year-old combat veteran who'd come back from Afghanistan with PTSD. He was a firefighter now, trying hard to conceal his condition, and he lived with his older brother in a house they would discover to be haunted. He was the character she and Tom had identified as the heartthrob on the show, the alpha male with a vulnerable side who would have women and girls swooning over him every week.

Luke shook his head. "Not Derek. James."

Kali stared at him. James Harding wasn't even a main character in the first season, although she had some cool ideas for his arc next year, assuming the network stuck with them that long. He was also a ghost.

She frowned. "James isn't a very showy character. He's the ghost of a young English teacher who falls in love with Alicia. He spends most of the first season pining for her."

"I know. But I like him. And you've given him a couple of amazing speeches, especially in later episodes. I bet you've got some cool stuff planned for him in the second season. Don't you?"

"Well . . . yes," she conceded. "But I just don't see you as James. He's in the background a lot of the time, overlooked by everyone—"

"Especially Alicia."

She sensed a trap, but since she didn't know what it was, she didn't know how to avoid it.

"Yes, especially Alicia. What's your point?"

"Being overlooked by the woman you love is a universal experience, something every guy can relate to. We've all experienced rejection at some point in our lives. Even me," he added with a grin. That got a laugh from most of the people in the room, but Kali flushed.

"Very funny. I'm just saying that casting you as James would be—"

"Going against type?"

"Well, yes."

"What was it you said this morning? That we can still be defined by whatever 'type' we were in high school, even years later? Sometimes going against type is the most powerful act of rebellion we have." He settled back in his chair. "Let's take you, for instance. What would you all say," he asked, glancing around the room, "if I told you that Kali came by my room last night to get naked and naughty?"

Good-natured laughter erupted, and her cheeks flamed as she leveled a glare at Luke that should have vaporized him.

He grinned at her unrepentantly. "That would be going against type for you, right? But it might be good for you. I sure as hell know it would be good for me."

She took a deep breath and tried to reclaim control of the situation. "Fine, whatever. Go ahead and read for James. Do you need a scene partner?"

He shook his head. "No, the speech I have in mind is a monologue—the one where he first tells Alicia how he feels about her. Just to give you a sense of how I might do in the role."

She expected him to make an introductory speech, give them some kind of lead in. But he just looked down at the script, flipped to the page he was looking for, and started to read. His voice was quiet, thoughtful, almost matter-of-fact.

"I died more than fifty years ago. Even back then, I thought the problem with our society was that we were too damn busy. And it's a thousand times worse now. People run around like ants, and why? For what?

"Do you want to know the one advantage to being a ghost? Time. I have time to read, time to watch sunsets. Time to float through walls, which is a highly underrated activity. Time to think. Time to pay attention. And in all those years, I've only found one person I thought was worth paying attention to. That's you, Alicia.

"I watch you. Some days I watch you for hours. I know I probably shouldn't, but I can't seem to help myself. You have this stillness about you when you're sitting and thinking, a stillness I hardly ever see in the living.

"When you're reading a book you love, your emotions show on your face. That happens when you're playing the piano, too, or walking by yourself. You're much more guarded when you're with people. When you were younger, before you learned how to protect yourself, you said what you thought and spoke from your heart—and sometimes people laughed at you. It hurt, and so you don't do that anymore.

"I know you're in love with Max, and it kills me. Of course I understand why. He's confident, he's outgoing, he always knows what to say in social situations. You're drawn to him because things that are hard for you are easy for him.

"But he'll never look into your heart. If you end up dating, you'll never be more than a sweet, pretty girl to him. If you end up married, you'll be the sweet, pretty girl he married. He'll never look any further. He'll never know you to the roots of your soul. He'll never see the vistas in your mind, the visions that fill your consciousness until the only outlet is your piano or your journal or your dreams.

"I see all of that. I see it, and it makes me want you like I've never wanted anything. I ache for you. I hunger for you. When I'm near you, I feel alive again.

"You know that book you loved when you were little? *The Velveteen Rabbit?* Sometimes you still pull it off the shelf and read it, holding it carefully because it's so old and worn. I used to think it was a silly story. Childish and sentimental. But that was before I had ever loved someone the way I love you. Before I knew that love does make us real.

"Loving you is changing me, Alicia. I don't know yet what I'm becoming, but I feel myself letting go of what I was. I don't know if I have a place in this world, or in your life. All I ask is that you let me haunt you once in a while."

Luke finished reading, and laid the script down on the table. For a minute no one said a word.

Kali's skin prickled with goose bumps. She wrapped her arms around her waist, hugging herself, and at the slight movement Luke turned his head and looked at her.

Her throat ached and her eyes stung as emotion tried to escape her body.

It wasn't just that he'd done an amazing job with that speech. She was also remembering with a pang of loss the communion she'd felt when they collaborated—at fourteen when they were at summer camp and then at eighteen, when they'd worked on the senior play together. The times when she wrote words and Luke brought them to life had been the happiest of her life. He always got her so thoroughly, understood so instinctively what she was trying to say. And he always found more in her scripts than she'd intended to put there, drawing out nuances of thought and emotion she hadn't been consciously aware of.

When they'd worked together, they'd been more than just the sum of their parts.

How had such a partnership been destroyed? How had the two of them been blown so far apart that they hadn't spoken in ten years?

Because romance had come into the picture. It had been one variable too many in their fragile human equation, and it had wrecked the balance between them.

They should have stuck to work and friendship. If they had, they might have found ways to collaborate over the years. Projects they could have worked on together. Or, if Luke's Hollywood career didn't leave time for that, they could have at least stayed in touch. She could have sent him her scripts to get his feedback, and he could have talked to her about his movie choices. Maybe she could have convinced him to do a few indie films in the midst of all his blockbusters.

But what good was it to think about what might have been?

The reality was, they wouldn't be working together on *Ghosts*. She'd be the biggest fool in the world if she believed that Luke would abandon his movie career to come to New York and act in her little show.

And nothing would happen between them romantically. The game they'd been playing was just that—a game. It didn't mean anything. A little leftover tension from high school, that was all.

She'd been frowning down at the table, and now she looked up to meet Luke's blue eyes.

A sudden shiver went through her.

Whatever their game had turned into, it had to end now. Because while she was sure it didn't mean anything to him, there was a chance . . . a small chance . . . that it was starting to mean something to her.

"That was incredible," the show's production designer said. Now that the silence was broken, other voices echoed the praise with excited enthusiasm.

Kali recognized the look in her colleagues' eyes, and her heart sank. They wanted him on the show. He'd brought magic into the room, and they wanted more.

She felt exhausted at the prospect of trying to rein in their enthusiasm. She couldn't deal with this right now; she just couldn't.

"What did you think, Kali?" Luke asked quietly.

"Could you see me playing James on the show?"

Yes, she could. After today, she'd never be able to see anyone else in the role.

That was the problem. She could see him on the show, and she could see him in her life—and neither of those things would ever really happen.

The lump was back in her throat, and she rose hastily to her feet. "That was a great reading, Luke. Thank you. Unfortunately, I need to—I—I'm feeling a little under the weather. Hannah, I wonder if you wouldn't mind taking over this meeting? And if someone would take notes for me, that would be very helpful."

Without waiting for a response, she hurried from the room.

* * *

She'd run away. Again.

He knew they had some baggage to deal with, but he was starting to get tired of Kali's disappearing act every time things got a little intense between them.

Enough was enough. Reading her words out loud today had reminded him of the connection they'd once shared . . . a connection he still felt.

He'd bet everything he owned that Kali felt it, too. And tonight they were going to talk about it.

He stopped at her room before dinner, but either she'd gone down already or she wasn't answering his knock. Either way, the only thing he could do was go down alone.

When he snapped at an autograph-seeker in the elevator, he knew he wouldn't be good for a damn thing until he confronted Kali. Until he made her admit that there was something between them. Something real.

He spotted her in the dining room almost immediately. She was sitting at a table with some of the people from her meeting today, and he saw with a surge of anger that she was flirting with the guy on her right.

Some might have thought she was simply talking to him, but Luke knew better. He might have gone ten years without seeing her but he still knew Kali better than any woman on the planet. She was flirting deliberately and a little anxiously, because she hardly ever flirted and she wasn't sure of herself.

And because she wasn't sure of herself she had no idea that she was, in fact, doing such a bang-up job that the guy—Eric, he thought—was staring at her with doglike devotion. Luke would have felt sorry for him if he wasn't so pissed off.

Apparently walking away from him again and again wasn't enough. Kali had now decided to attach herself to some other man as a way to put distance between them.

As though she felt the same magnetic pull that he did, her head turned and she met his eyes. She turned hastily away again, leaning towards Eric and putting a hand on his knee.

Luke's hands clenched into fists. He stood there for a moment, and then he turned around and walked away.

He went back to his suite and ordered a steak from room service, but instead of eating he paced back and forth, his emotions ratcheting up with every step.

It was good that he'd left the dining room. That was the wrong time and place to say to Kali what he needed to say. But after dinner, the network had reserved one of the patios outside for cocktails. She'd be fair game then.

On the dot of nine he was outside, prowling around the patio like a caged animal. People started to filter through the French doors that opened out from the dining room, mellow from dinner and ready for drinks.

There she was. She was still with Eric, her hand on his arm and her expression more relaxed—probably because he hadn't been at dinner and she thought she was safe.

She was wearing a green silk dress, and Luke was willing to bet Tom had picked this one out, too. It clung to her slender curves like it had been made for her, the neckline low enough to show the enticing valley between her breasts, and when Eric shot a look in that direction something snapped inside him.

Eric's quick glance at Kali's cleavage wasn't a monumental event in the grand scheme of things, but it was enough to push him over the edge. A primal voice howled that Kali was his, that no other man could look at her that way.

He knew his reaction was sexist as hell but he didn't care. As Luke strode across the patio towards them, all the tension and frustration of the last two days coalesced into a fierce rush of carnal intent.

Kali and Eric were at the bar now, facing away from him. He put a hand on Kali's shoulder and she jumped, spinning around to face him.

"Luke," she said blankly.

Eric turned, too. Oblivious to the tension crackling in the air, he stuck out his hand with a big smile. "That was a great reading today. I really hope you end up working with us on *Ghosts*. Hannah and I were saying that you really captured the—"

"Yeah. Do you mind if I borrow Kali for a minute?"

Eric blinked. "Uh—"

"Thanks."

He circled a hand around Kali's wrist, and then he was pulling her after him across the patio and onto the walkway that led to one of the outdoor pools. The pool area was dark and deserted, and the shed where the towels were kept would give them all the privacy he needed.

CHAPTER 6

Kali's heart was in her throat as Luke pulled her along after him, his grip on her wrist almost hard enough to hurt.

All of her consciousness was on that point of contact between them. There was something there that she wanted. Something that called to her on a wordless, primitive level.

He opened the door to a small shed and pulled her inside. As he kicked the door shut and crowded her back against the shelves, something happened to her body that she'd never experienced before.

She felt herself go pliant.

The shed was dark, but moonlight filtered down through two windows and a skylight. Luke loomed above her, his face hard and angular in the shadows, and now he put his arms on either side of her shoulders, caging her with his body.

There were stacks of towels behind her, and when she tilted her head back to look at him she felt their softness. It was an echo of the softness in her body, a voluptuous euphoria that bloomed inside her.

No truth or dare this time. Just an order.

"Turn around."

His voice was low and rough and commanding, and everything in her thrilled to the sound of it.

She obeyed instantly, heart pounding, as though she'd been waiting for Luke to tell her what to do since she was fourteen years old. She pressed her face into the towels, relishing their scent and texture.

Desire prickled her skin as Luke lowered her zipper. He pushed the dress down her body, letting it fall to the floor.

Then his hand was at her bra. With one deft twist he undid the clasp, tugging the straps down her arms and tossing it aside.

When he slid his thumbs into the elastic of her panties she started to shake. She wanted this—oh, God, she wanted this—but all her old fears and insecurities seemed to rise up at once and paralyze her.

Her panties were down. "Step out of them," Luke ordered her.

His voice cut through her fear. She did as he told her, lifting one foot and then the other. She was naked now except for her high heels. She closed her eyes tightly, her hands gripping the shelf in front of her.

He leaned close and whispered in her ear. "I've wanted you for so long, Kali. There wasn't a night senior year I didn't fantasize about you."

She felt his hands on her shoulders, big and strong and warm. His breath tickled her, and a feathery chill ghosted over her skin.

"As your friend I felt so much tenderness for you, so much gentleness. But when I dreamed about fucking you I was never gentle. When you stood me up on prom night, I thought maybe you'd sensed it somehow. That you knew how I fantasized about you and didn't want anything to do with me.

"Of course that was just one of the things I thought. I went through every possibility in my head. Sometimes I thought it was because of your dad, or because I was poor."

Then, as though the memory of those days made him want to stake a claim on her body, he slid a hand down to her pussy and pushed three fingers inside her.

She gasped at the rough invasion, and his fingers began to rotate slowly, stretching her.

"You're so fucking tight," he said, his voice as rough as his touch. He slid his other hand around her and then up, cupping her left breast and pinching her nipple.

She moaned then, her body twisting restlessly in his grasp.

"After prom night, I swore I'd never fantasize about you again. Sometimes I'd even last a week or two. But then . . . you know that moment when you're masturbating, when you're close and you just need something, some image, to push you over the edge?"

Yes, she knew that moment. Luke had inhabited that place in her psyche since she'd first figured out how to give herself an orgasm.

He moved closer, and for the first time let her feel his erection. He pushed his cock against her and she arched back into him, the movement increasing the friction of his fingers inside her.

"When I can't control my thoughts any more, I think of you. You've pushed me over the edge so many times that just thinking about you can get me hard."

He pulled his hands from her body, and she almost cried out in protest.

Then he spoke into her ear again, softer than before. And though he wasn't touching her at all she felt him behind her like an impending force—a flame or a tide or a predator, ready to consume her.

"Here's the thing, Kali. You deserve a partner who'll make love to you exactly the way you want. The way you need. If what you want is a gentle, considerate lover, then I'm not your man. I could be for any other woman on the planet, but not you. What I feel for you is too intense."

He put his hands on her again, gripping her hips and pulling her towards him. "If that freaks you out or scares you, tell me now. Tell me now and I'll let you go. Otherwise I'm going to fuck you exactly the way I want to. And it won't be gentle."

Every word he'd said illuminated the dark, formless place inside her until she felt transparent, filled with heat and light and knowledge. Had she sensed this about him all along? Yearned for it without understanding it?

Because this was what she wanted—this hard possessiveness, this fierce passion. Her own timidity and uncertainty about sex, which other men had responded to with patience and respect and gentle courtship, burned away like straw in the face of Luke's dominance.

But she didn't know how to say that out loud. So she turned instead, pressing her naked body to his clothed one and burying her face against his chest.

"Luke," was all she could manage, her voice muffled against his body.

It was enough.

He slid his hands into her hair and urged her head back. He looked down at her for one burning instant, and then his mouth was on hers.

His kiss was an assault that left her breathless and boneless. One hand moved to the back of her head as the other slid down to cup her ass, holding her against his erection. His tongue circled hers, taking possession, and the heat and friction made her moan against his mouth.

He pulled back suddenly. "Spread your legs."

Her knees were like jelly but she managed it somehow, widening her stance and wondering why he—

Oh, God. He dropped to a crouch in front of her, and he was staring at her pussy like it was the most beautiful thing he'd ever seen. She remembered last night, touching herself in front of him, and how Luke's eyes on her had made her so hot she thought she'd combust.

He used his thumbs to open her wide, the cool air on her hidden flesh making her shiver.

"Do you want my mouth?" he asked, looking up at her.

Was he giving her a choice? "I—I've never really been comfortable with—"

He leaned forward and licked her, the flat of his tongue like wet velvet.

She squeaked, and then she felt rather than heard his chuckle, a low vibration against her body.

No choice, then. The thought made her dizzy with pleasure.

He dug in deeper, spreading her wider. She'd never been this open, this exposed. The hard pressure of his thumbs was half pleasure, half pain, while his tongue was a soft seduction, teasing sensation from her as he explored her secret places.

I'm yours.

It was the answer to what he was doing to her, the claim he was staking. Surrender was in her very bones, in the arch of her spine as her body rippled with desire. She would open to him utterly. She would give him whatever he wanted.

She slid her hands into his hair as he drove her higher, his tongue thrusting inside her. And now his thumb was on her clitoris and she was so close, so close.

Then his hands gripped her hips and his mouth was everywhere, devouring and consuming, licking and sucking and biting. When she felt his teeth on her aching clit the sudden pain ignited an orgasm that ripped through her body. As she cried out his name, only his hands on her hips kept her from falling to the ground.

She still hadn't fully recovered when Luke rose to his feet.

"Take off my clothes," he said, his voice rough.

God, yes. She started undoing buttons, her hands shaking and clumsy, and when she'd finished she swept the shirt open and pressed her lips to his chest. He put a hand to the back of her head, holding her there for a second. Then he pulled back.

"Keep going."

She undid his belt and pulled it loose. Then she lowered his zipper, revealing black boxers stretched over his erection, which was as long and thick and hard as she'd always imagined.

"You're not done," he reminded her. She fumbled at his waist and pulled his pants and boxers down together, and after he'd kicked off his shoes he stepped free of his clothes and stood there, big and powerful and naked and aroused, and she wanted to touch and taste him more than she'd ever wanted anything in her life.

"Take me in your mouth," he said, and when she knelt down she relished the rough floor against her knees and the cool air on her skin and the sudden ache in her still-wet pussy as she wrapped her hand around the base of his cock and swirled her tongue around him.

God, he was big. She'd never been a size-matters girl before, but Luke had just changed her mind.

He cupped the back of her head as she took as much of him as she could, and a rush of pleasure sang along her nerves. When his hand pressed harder, forcing her to take him deeper, her pussy throbbed in response.

Then suddenly he pulled away.

He was still for a moment, and Kali sensed him fighting for control. Then he grabbed a handful of towels and tossed them on the floor.

"On your back," he told her. He reached for his pants, grabbing his wallet from the pocket. "Spread your legs."

She lay down in a nest of towels as Luke pulled out a condom and tore it open.

"Please," she said, suddenly desperate to have him inside her. "Please."

He dropped to his knees, his eyes meeting hers in the moonlight. "You're so beautiful. And I've wanted you for so long."

"I've wanted you, too. I've never wanted anything more."

His hands gripped her thighs. "Wider," he said, spreading her legs as far apart as they would go, sending a throb of pleasure through her at the helplessness of her position.

He settled over her then, supporting his weight on his arms as his head dipped down to her breasts. His mouth teased her nipples as his cock teased her pussy, pressing against her without penetration until she almost screamed.

He kissed his way up to her neck as she writhed beneath him, trying to arch herself onto his cock.

"Beg for it," he said, his mouth against her throat.

"Please, Luke. Please—"

"Please what?"

"Fuck me!"

He invaded her body with one powerful stroke, burying himself inside her and staying there, grinding against her clit until she clutched at his knotted arms.

"Oh, God, Luke—"

He began to move then, pulling out and pushing back in, and he was so big and hard and perfect she dug her nails into his biceps.

His head jerked up when he felt her claw at him. And suddenly he was pounding into her, his expression raw and fierce and exultant.

"Kali," he said over and over again. "Kali."

Her climax hit like a tsunami. She threw her head back as she called out Luke's name, and he slammed into her one more time before he stiffened with his own orgasm, his body shuddering with aftershocks as he collapsed on top of her.

It took a long, long time to come back to earth.

She had never felt like this before. She was floating in a golden haze, her body buzzing and humming. Luke's head was buried against her shoulder, and she threaded her fingers into his hair in a spasm of tenderness.

"Mmmmm," he said, a low rumble of pleasure that vibrated against her skin.

He shifted much sooner than she was ready for him to, and she murmured in protest.

"I'm too heavy," he told her, rolling onto his side and pulling her with him, cradling her against his chest.

His arms tightened around her as she nestled against him.

"That was incredible," she said, still boneless with pleasure.

Luke hesitated before answering. "It wasn't too rough?"

"God, no." She thought about that for a moment. "I wonder what that says about me. Do you think I feel some deep inner need to be dominated and will require years of expensive therapy?"

He laughed then, a rich, happy sound that reverberated through both their bodies.

"What's so funny?" she asked suspiciously, even though it was impossible to keep from smiling with him.

"Nothing. Nothing. I—" he stopped suddenly. "I feel very, uh, fond of you right now," he finished, and Kali knew with a thrill of certainty what he'd stopped himself from saying.

"You didn't answer my question," she said, pressing a kiss into his breastbone.

He smoothed a hand into the dip of her waist and up the curve of her hip. "I think you have a very specific need to be dominated by me sexually . . . just like I have a very specific need to dominate you sexually. But you'd never let me dominate you any other way and I would never try. You can run circles around me intellectually, and emotionally . . ." He paused. "I guess I'd say we're equals. Not that that's saying much."

"What do you mean?"

"Well . . . I don't think either one of us can lay claim to much emotional maturity. Not when we've never let go of the past." There was a note of determination in his voice, and Kali felt her muscles tensing as she sensed what was coming.

This time, though, she wasn't going to run.

Luke pulled back so he could look her in the eyes.

"Truth or dare?" he asked.

"Truth."

CHAPTER 7

As he looked down at Kali lying in the circle of his arms, a surge of love and protectiveness went through him that had nothing to do with the mind-blowing sex they'd just experienced.

They belonged together. He'd never been so sure of anything in his life. But before they looked to the future, they needed to put the past behind them for good.

"Why did you stand me up on prom night?"

Kali took a deep breath. "I can't believe it took us ten years to have this conversation."

He brushed the back of his knuckles across her cheekbone. "Better late than never. Was it your dad? Did he say you couldn't go with me?"

She nodded. "That was part of it. He said . . ." She paused, and he could see her face tense with the memories. "It was after Lisa James accused you of being the father of her baby. Do you remember that?"

It wasn't something he could ever forget. The situation with Lisa had changed him, had made him think more seriously than he ever had before about his relationships with girls, and the possible consequences—not just for him, but for them.

"Yeah, I remember."

"You told me you'd always used protection when you were with her, and I believed you. And of course Lisa admitted later that you weren't the father. But that was after the prom. Before the truth came out, when everyone still thought it was you, my dad said . . ." She paused again. "He said you were trash, that all you were interested in was sex, that you'd screw me and dump me just like you'd dumped Lisa."

It wasn't a surprise, but it still stung. Not just because of what Kali's father had said, but because it reminded him of the way he'd felt about himself then. His own father, Kali's father, the way everyone had been so quick to condemn him . . . it had all been a confirmation of how he felt about himself, deep inside.

Maybe that's why he hadn't fought harder for Kali back then. Because on some level, he didn't think he deserved her.

"Did you believe him?"

Kali shook her head. "I didn't think you were trash, or that all you wanted from me was sex. But . . ."

"But what?"

"I knew how many girls you'd been with. And you always broke up with them, never the other way around. It was hard for me to imagine that I could ever . . . I don't know, hold your interest. And the sex part . . ." She hesitated. "After you kissed me that day, I knew . . . I felt . . . that you wanted me. And that was absolutely terrifying. I wanted you too, more than I'd ever wanted anything. I'd always had a crush on you. But I was so inexperienced, so awkward and hopeless about guy-girl stuff. At first I told myself it would be okay, that you would show me what to do. But then . . ."

"What?"

She sighed. "It's so humiliating to talk about things that seemed important back in high school. Saying it out loud makes it seem stupid, but the emotions back then were so powerful . . ."

"I know," he said softly. "And it's the emotions that we remember. That keep us from moving forward."

She sighed again. "Well. About a week before the prom, I overheard Jeff Crane and Mick Raleigh talking."

"I have a bad feeling already."

"Mick said he couldn't understand why you'd asked me to the prom. Jeff said you must be on a cherry-popping kick, but that you'd get bored with me after a week or so and be back in action."

"Assholes."

"Then you joined them, and—"

"Shit."

"They didn't say anything to you about me, specifically. They just started talking about sex, and how much better it is when you're with a girl who knows what she's doing. And you agreed."

"Shit," he said again. He shook his head. "I don't even remember that conversation."

She smiled up at him. "That's probably because you talked with your friends like that all the time. You were just shooting the breeze, the way teenage boys do. If they'd mentioned my name or insulted me, that would have been different, and you would have defended me. But at the time I didn't think of that. And I couldn't forget it no matter how much I tried. I didn't think you'd dump me, necessarily, after we had sex . . . but I thought you'd be bored. I thought you'd regret asking me out, and wish that we'd just stayed friends. And then . . ."

"It gets worse?"

"My dad said that if I promised not to see you again, he'd make sure you got that scholarship to UCLA—the one he was sponsoring. And if I kept seeing you, he'd make sure that you didn't . . . and he'd do everything he could to keep you from having a career in Hollywood."

"Jesus. What a—"

He stopped. What would he have done in her father's place, if he had a daughter like Kali?

He'd like to think he wouldn't have resorted to bribery or blackmail. But he would have done whatever he could to protect Kali from a guy like him . . . or the guy he'd seemed to be.

He ran a hand over his face.

"What is it?" Kali asked.

"I always suspected something like that. That's why I refused to take the scholarship when they told me I'd won it. Even if I'd earned it fair and square, I didn't want to take anything from your father."

Kali nodded. "I was so upset when I found out you'd turned it down. I felt like I'd made this huge sacrifice for nothing, and of course you didn't even know. But when I tried to talk to you about it, you—"

She stopped, and he winced. After Kali had stood him up on prom night, he'd cut her out of his life completely. He wouldn't even look at her in the hallways at school.

"I was such an asshole to you."

"I deserved it. I was a coward. I should have talked to you, should have told you what happened with my dad. We'd been such good friends up to that point . . . I'd always been able to tell you anything. That was the worst part, you know. Losing your friendship."

He caught the glitter of tears in her eyes, and he pulled her close. "Hey," he murmured into her hair. "You're never going to lose me again, okay? I swear it."

"I can't believe it still hurts so much to think about. I was so stupid back then, so—"

"That's all over, Kali. It's in the past. We're not the same people anymore. We're capable of things now that we weren't capable of then. At least, I hope we are. I'd hate to think we haven't learned a damn thing in ten years."

"But we messed things up so badly. We—"

"Yeah, we messed things up. But maybe we were doing the best we could. Even your dad. He was just trying to protect you, you know."

Kali pulled back and stared at him. "You're saying that you can forgive him?"

"Yeah. I can. I think what he did was lousy, but I understand why he did it." He paused. "What about you? Can you forgive him?"

She was silent a minute. "I never used to think so," she said finally. "But now . . . I'm not sure. We haven't spoken in so long. He's reached out to me a couple of times, and I've never responded. But maybe I should."

They held each other in silence for a minute, thinking about everything they'd talked about. Luke actually felt lighter, as though the ghost of the past had been clinging to his back, weighing him down.

"We still haven't finished the game," Kali said suddenly, raising herself up on one elbow.

He smiled at her. "We haven't?"

She shook her head. "Nope. I still have one more turn. So . . . truth or dare?"

"Truth."

"Okay. After your career started to take off, why did you make all those action movies? You have so much talent, so much passion. Why didn't you ever work on a project that would have brought that out?"

He grinned at her. "The truth? I wanted to make money. I wanted to make so much money that no one could ever look down on me again, or think of me as a charity case. Especially you."

"I never looked down on you, Luke. And I never thought of you as a charity case."

"I know that now, but I didn't then. After high school I was so angry with . . . well, pretty much everyone. My career in the beginning was one big *fuck you* to the world. And later, when I had enough money and box office clout to pick and choose my movies, I'd gotten into a rut. And nothing inspired me to get out of it."

Until you, he wanted to say—but there was a weight of expectation behind that statement that he wasn't sure Kali was ready for. He knew what he wanted: to leave L.A. and his Hollywood career and move to New York. To work with Kali on *Ghosts*, and to be with her.

But that was a lot of intensity to lay on her this soon. And he wasn't going to screw things up by rushing.

There would be plenty of time later to talk about the future.

He leaned over and pressed a kiss to her forehead. "As much as I've enjoyed spending time with these towels, what would you say to finishing the night in my bed?"

She smiled at him. "I'm tempted, but . . . I'm also feeling kind of overwhelmed. I could use some time to process. You know?"

No, he didn't. He didn't need time to process. But Kali was cautious when it came to matters of the heart, and he'd already promised himself not to rush her.

He kept his voice light, trying not to betray how much he hated this idea. "So . . . separate rooms tonight?"

"I think so. And then, tomorrow, we'll talk."

He rolled her onto her back and covered her with his body. "Just talk?"

He knew he was playing dirty, but he couldn't help it. There was a chance that once Kali's rational side took the reins, she'd try to push him away again. But right here, right now, she was his.

A surge of possessiveness rocketed through him. When tomorrow came, he and Kali would have a civilized discussion about their future. But there was nothing civilized about the chemistry between them.

"Fight me."

Her breath was coming in little pants as she gazed up at him. "What?"

"Try to fight me."

She stared at him, and for a moment he didn't think she'd do it. But then she began to struggle, her body twisting and her hands pushing against his chest. He felt her excitement in the sudden slickness of her pussy and the hardening of her nipples, and as he pinned her down with the weight of his body, his own excitement rose until he thought he'd explode then and there.

His wallet was on the floor beside them. He grabbed Kali's wrists in one hand and his wallet in the other, taking out the last remaining condom and tearing the foil open with his teeth. As he slid the latex sheath over his throbbing erection, Kali jerked one of her hands free and slapped him across the face.

She froze, stunned at what she'd done. Luke stared down at her, equally stunned, his cheek burning where she'd struck him.

And then savage arousal fired his blood.

He grabbed her wrists again, jerking them over her head and pinning them down. He pushed her thighs apart with his knee and drove into her hard and deep, astonished all over again at how tight she was, how hot and wet and perfect for him.

Kali cried out his name. He angled his thrusts to grind against her clit, and her legs wrapped around his waist as her head thrashed from side to side. He drove her mercilessly until he felt her body tighten and flutter around him, and in the next instant his own climax seared his nerve endings and melted his bones, his cock spasming as he buried himself inside her.

For a minute, all he could hear was the pounding of his heart and the rush of blood in his ears. When he could function again, he kissed Kali's forehead, her cheeks, her lips.

I love you.

But he couldn't say it in the afterglow of great sex. They were amazing together, and he wasn't sorry that he'd just reminded her of that fact . . . but he wouldn't use it against her. Sex was only part of the equation between them.

But he wasn't a saint. When Kali said, "My God, that was incredible," he kissed her again and said, "Just something for you to think about when you're alone in your bed tonight."

* * *

Just something for you to think about when you're alone in your bed tonight.

As if she could think about anything else.

Sleeping in her own room had seemed like such a rational, sensible idea when she thought of it. She needed some distance, didn't she? When Luke was touching her, her body overwhelmed her brain. And there'd been moments when she'd felt such intense tenderness and affection towards him that she'd scared herself. It was all too much, too fast. She needed time to make sense of everything.

Of course now that she was in bed, alone, all she could do was toss and turn and think about Luke.

And then the doubts came flooding in.

Luke had a life in L.A., and she had a life in New York. Long-distance relationships were tough under the best circumstances, and you could hardly call these the best.

She'd have to be crazy to believe she would be enough for Luke in the long term. That he would resist all the temptations of his Hollywood life—all the women throwing themselves at him on a daily basis—for the privilege of seeing her a few times a year. Did she really think she was that special? That Luke would ever—

Suddenly she sat straight up in bed.

She was thinking the same exact things she'd thought back in high school.

She was running herself down . . . and Luke, too. She was making assumptions about her own worth, and about what Luke wanted, that had no basis in reality.

And just like in high school, she was making a decision about the two of them without giving Luke a say. Because she was afraid.

She was afraid of being rejected. Of not being enough.

And then, slowly, a single question surfaced in her mind.

Would being rejected be the worst thing in the world?

No. It wouldn't. Being too much of a coward to go after what she wanted—*that* would be the worst thing in the world.

She lifted the phone receiver from its cradle and dialed Luke's room. It only took two rings for him to pick up.

"Yeah?"

"It's me," she said, her heart beating ridiculously fast.

"Hey, you," he answered, his voice so warm and deep and rich that a tingle ran through her body. "What's up? Can't sleep?"

She shook her head, and then remembered they were on the phone. "Nope." She hesitated a moment, and then came out with it. "I miss you."

He chuckled, and the tingle turned into a full-fledged shiver. "You do, huh? It's only been an hour since we said goodnight."

"I know. I . . ." She took a deep breath, and stepped off the cliff. "I wanted to tell you that I . . . want to be with you. If that's something that you want. I know it'll be tough, living so far apart, but we could—"

"Kali."

For one horrible moment, her heart stopped beating. Oh, God, she'd been wrong. Being rejected *would* be the worst thing in the world.

She cleared her throat. "I shouldn't have called like this. I'm sorry. I—"

"Kali. Shut up a second, would you?"

She shut up.

"I've been lying here in bed thinking about you, and wondering how the hell I was going to stop myself from rushing things. I was so scared I was going to screw everything up by going too fast. But now . . ." He paused. "We didn't tell each other what we wanted ten years ago, and I'm not going to make that mistake again. I want to be with you, too. I want to work with you on *Ghosts*. I want to move to New York City and ask you out on a lot of dates. And after a few months of that, I'm going to ask you to marry me in the most cheesy, romantic, over-the-top way I can think of."

Her eyes squeezed shut as a tidal wave of happiness crashed over her.

"You can't be thinking about marriage," she said breathlessly. "We're just starting to get to know each other again."

"Yeah, I know. That's why we'll go on all the dates first."

"But you talked about marriage like it's a foregone conclusion."

"It is. I'd ask you to marry me right now, but I figure you'll need a few months before you're sure. Plus, that'll give me time to come up with the perfect proposal."

She hadn't known it was possible for the human heart to contain this much joy. "What if I have special requests? You know, like doves or swans or clowns?"

"You want clowns at your marriage proposal?"

"Well, sure. That way, if someone happens to sing 'Send in the clowns,' I'll be able to say 'Don't worry, they're here.'"

He laughed then, a full-on belly laugh, and Kali found herself grinning at the receiver.

"It's not every action movie star who would get a Sondheim reference, you know," he told her.

"I know. That's why I love you, Luke. Because you go against type."

A beat went by. "Say that again."

She couldn't seem to stop smiling. "You mean about you going against type?"

"No, the other thing."

"I would, but . . ."

"But what?"

"I'd rather do it in person. Also, I'd rather do it naked."

Another beat. "Give me two minutes," he said, and then she heard a dial tone.

Forty-five seconds later, he was at her door.

As Luke scooped her up and carried her to the bed, she had a sudden vision of what her future would be like with this man.

And for the first time, she knew that real life was better than any story she could ever imagine.

ONLY DESIRE

CHAPTER 1

Lucy Barnaby stared up at the flashing neon sign. It announced "Sexy Nude Ladies" in a garish shade of purple, and since this section of Waikiki catered to both American and Japanese tourists, she figured the kanji characters beside the English words were a Japanese translation of "Sexy Nude Ladies".

What on God's green earth had made her think she'd have the guts to go through with this insane plan? Until tonight, the most risqué thing Lucy had ever done was go to a midnight showing of *The Rocky Horror Picture Show*.

Two women chattering together brushed past her as they went into the club. On their way to work, probably. One of them was tanned and blonde and curvy; the other was pale and Asian and flat-chested.

That made Lucy feel a little better. Maybe her own modest B cups wouldn't be as out-of-place as she'd feared.

If she went through with this.

Monday night at seven o'clock was when Sheila, the club's manager, held auditions for new dancers. When Lucy had spoken to her yesterday, she'd said that Lucy would probably be the only girl trying out tonight. At the time, Lucy thought that was a good thing—there wouldn't be anyone else to compare herself to. But now, seeing those confident, experienced dancers heading in to work, Lucy wished she weren't the only newbie here.

She checked her watch; five after seven. It was now or never. Was she going in there to take her clothes off, or what?

A group of college-aged guys stopped a few yards away and looked at the club.

"I've never been in here. Anybody know if the girls are fine?"

"Yeah, they're pretty decent, but it's a no-touching club. They don't do lap dances or anything like that. I'm in the mood to shoot in my pants, so let's go around the corner."

Shoot in his *pants*? Was that what really happened during a lap dance?

Her housemate Jessica worked at a lap dance club. She'd described what she did as "jacking men off with their clothes on", but somehow, Lucy hadn't really thought that guys could actually come like that. Maybe they got turned on, but could they actually ejaculate in public?

Okay, that decided it. This definitely wasn't her world. Even though this particular club didn't do lap dances, there were bound to be other things she hadn't thought about that she wasn't ready for and couldn't deal with. She was an anthropology grad student who'd slept with exactly three guys in her life, and she'd never even been adventurous enough to leave the light on during sex. She must have been out of her mind to think she—

"You guys go ahead. I'm heading home to Malia," one of the college kids said.

"Man, you're pussy-whipped." That was the first guy, shaking his head.

The other one just grinned. "Why go out for hamburger when you've got filet mignon at home?"

"I can't believe you're still hooked on that girl. You've been going out for two years. What's the big attraction?"

"It's pretty simple, really. The sex is incredible."

"Still?"

"I swear to God, it gets better every time. Malia is the wildest girl I've ever been with. My old girlfriend wouldn't even let me turn the light on during sex, and the other day Malia and I did it in an elevator. Her idea."

"Holy shit."

"I know."

The group of guys were walking away now, and Lucy couldn't hear any more of their conversation. But what she had heard was enough to change her mind about going inside that club.

"My old girlfriend wouldn't even let me turn the light on during sex."

He might as well have been dating *her*. Boring, conventional, tame Lucy Barnaby.

Wasn't that what Keenan had said last week?

She pictured the scene in her mind. She and her three housemates had been in the kitchen making dinner, which had started off really fun—she and Keenan were in charge of the salad, and they'd made their prep work into a competition, racing to see who could chop their carrots first, and then the mushrooms and peppers and zucchini. When they finished at the same time they decided to break the tie by seeing who could catch more croutons in their mouths when Sami tossed them from the kitchen table.

She'd been laughing so hard she hadn't even caught one. Keenan pumped his fist in the air when he beat her, and she swore to get her revenge the next time they played *Call of Duty*.

It was a great evening—until Jessica started talking about fixing Lucy up with a guy she knew from school, a football player named Hiro.

Keenan shook his head. "I know that guy. There's no way he and Lucy would hit it off."

Jessica frowned. "Why not?"

"He's looking for someone a little more . . ."

"A little more what?"

"A little more exciting."

Jessica and Sami both responded indignantly.

"Are you saying Lucy's not exciting?"

"Any guy would be lucky to have her!"

It was sweet of her friends to defend her. But Lucy herself hadn't been able to say a word.

She and Keenan argued a lot, and she'd never been shy about taking him on. But this was different. This wasn't a friendly disagreement about sports or politics or current events. This got at one of her deepest insecurities about herself, and anything she might have said stuck in her throat.

Keenan shrugged off his housemates. "I don't think Lucy's boring, but she's not exactly a risk-taker. Especially when it comes to relationships."

"What's that supposed to mean?" Jessica demanded.

Keenan looked at Lucy with one eyebrow up and a half-smile on his face. "Come on. Don't you remember her last boyfriend? The bug guy?"

"Entomologist," Lucy said through gritted teeth, finally able to get a word out.

"If that guy represents Lucy's speed, I'd say she's definitely in the slow class. And that was eight months ago. Since then, nothing. And do you remember last month when Sami put that porno on? She turned beet red and had to leave the room. And what about the night we were talking about sex toys? I've never seen a girl look so embarrassed."

It was at that point that Lucy had gotten up from the kitchen table and left the house. Jessica had called after her, but she got into her car and drove away before anyone could stop her.

Damn Keenan Diaz. Damn him, damn him, damn him to hell.

She remembered the sex toy conversation, all right. And yes, she'd been embarrassed . . . but not for the reason he thought.

She'd been embarrassed because at one point in the conversation Keenan had talked about bondage, and she'd been so suddenly and unexpectedly turned on it felt like her body was on fire.

Well, at least now she knew the answer to one question that had been worrying her ever since. Keenan obviously had no idea she'd been turned on by the idea of him tying a woman up . . . or that she was turned on by *him*.

He obviously thought she was too tame to be turned on by anything.

A couple of days after that conversation, Lucy started calling strip clubs. Only a few said they were looking for new dancers, and she decided to audition at *Centerfolds* because the woman she spoke to sounded nice over the phone, and because it wasn't one of the clubs that Keenan went to every so often.

She'd debated whether to go through with it all day, until Keenan came back from a run and jumped in the shower. A few minutes later he was heading out again.

"Where are you going?" Sami called from the kitchen. "Dinner's in two hours."

"I'll be back by then. I'm going to see Nikki."

"Why don't you ever bring your girls here, man?"

Keenan grinned. "The walls in this place aren't too thick. I'd hate for any of my sweet, innocent housemates to hear anything that might embarrass them."

That little dig, along with the unwelcome image of Keenan with another girl, had made up Lucy's mind for her. She was going to do it. For one night—and maybe more, if she didn't make a total fool of herself—she was going to be a sexy vixen instead of a nerdy grad student. For one night, she was going to be wild.

The door to the club opened, and a scrawny guy with a receding hairline and a wispy goatee came out. For a second she thought he was a customer, but then she saw the *Centerfolds* logo on his shirt. The doorman, probably.

He noticed her looking at him.

"Are you going in, sweetheart?"

"Yes," she said quickly, before she could chicken out.

He held the door for her. "The club's upstairs," he said. "Good luck," he added, which was nice. But as she went past him and started up the carpeted staircase, she heard him mutter to himself, "That one won't last five minutes."

Lucy paused for just a moment before continuing on her way. Maybe he was right, but that wasn't going to stop her from trying. For just once in her life she wanted to do something crazy and daring. So what if she made a fool of herself?

She thought of the quote Sami had taped above his desk.

You will do foolish things, but do them with enthusiasm.

That was the spirit.

Music came from behind the door at the top of the stairs. She opened it and found herself in a large, dimly-lit space with three stages—complete with stripper poles, naturally—and a zinc-topped bar at the far end.

It was early on a Monday night and the club wasn't crowded. Only one of the stages was lit, and a few dozen men were scattered around it. Three dancers were gyrating to the music, smiling down at the men gazing up at them.

Lucy moved closer, keeping to the shadows around the edges of the room. One of the dancers was African-

American, one was a redhead, and one was Polynesian. All three were topless but wearing g-strings, which was a relief. At least she wouldn't have to get totally naked.

Of more interest—to Lucy, anyway—were the garters the girls wore around their thighs. They were so stuffed with dollar bills they looked like Christmas wreaths, and for the first time it occurred to her that there might be more than one reason to give this stripper thing a try. She received a stipend from the University in exchange for working as a teaching assistant, but like most grad students she lived pretty close to the bone. A little extra income would come in handy.

Of course that was assuming that

1. She went through with auditioning;
2. She didn't make a complete idiot of herself; and
3. Sheila wanted to hire her.

At the moment, only the first item on the list seemed remotely possible.

She took a deep breath and studied the dancers. Their moves didn't seem that complicated—hip thrusts, some sexy swaying and posturing, and the occasional swing around the pole. She'd taken years of dance classes and she was specializing in dance ethnology at the University. She could probably manage to do what those girls were doing. It really didn't seem too—

Then the song ended and another began. This one was slower and sexier, and all three dancers, using their own unique moves, slid their g-strings down and off.

They were naked now. Totally naked.

Did she have the guts to go the full Monty?

Except for garters and shoes, of course.

The shoes might be an issue. Lucy had brought her highest heels, but they were only three inches. The girls up there were wearing five-inch spikes, and the redhead was wearing a pair of platform pumps that looked more like six inches.

She wasn't tall to begin with. Wouldn't she look like a midget compared to—

"Are you the new girl?"

Lucy turned her head to see an Asian woman peering at her with her hands on her hips. Sheila, she presumed.

"Um . . . yes."

The woman looked her up and down. "It's good that you're blonde. The Japanese tourist season is starting to ramp up and they like blondes. Ever done any dancing before?"

"Ballet and tap, and I've been studying hula for the last two years."

Sheila frowned at her. "I mean this kind of dancing."

"Oh. No."

"Any other kind of sexy work? Peep shows, maybe? Or a masturbation booth?"

Masturbation booth? What the heck was a masturbation booth? Who did the masturbating?

"No."

Sheila hadn't asked about her experience over the phone. Was that going to be enough to disqualify her? And if it was, would she be relieved or disappointed?

Sheila seemed to be considering the same question. Finally she huffed out a quick, sharp sigh.

"Well, we need girls. I might as well take a look at you. Go ahead and change and then find me at the bar. The dressing room's that way," she added, jerking her head towards a small door on her left.

Without waiting for a response, she turned on her heel and marched away.

Lucy looked after her for a moment. Then she looked at the dancers again. And then, for the first time, she looked at the men sitting around the stage.

They didn't look critical or contemptuous. They looked enraptured.

It occurred to Lucy that she might be overestimating what men look for in a naked woman. It was possible that the simple fact of nakedness—helped by makeup, high heels, and the flattering low light of the club—was enough to overcome a girl's flaws.

There was only one way to find out.

CHAPTER 2

Back home, Keenan grabbed a beer from the refrigerator and put a piece of Sami's homemade spam and pineapple pizza on a paper plate.

He was in a rotten mood. He'd gone over to Nikki's hoping for a little mindless but satisfying sex, and ended up breaking up with her instead.

Although *breaking up* wasn't really the right phrase. You had to be in a relationship to break up, and for the last year Keenan had enforced a strict no-relationship policy.

He told everyone it was because he wasn't looking for anything serious and wanted to be upfront about that fact. He could only pray that no one suspected the real reason he didn't do relationships anymore.

Because he was totally, hopelessly, head-over-fucking-heels in love with Lucy Barnaby.

But since they would never work as a couple, he intended to keep those feelings to himself for the duration—which meant until she moved back to the mainland after she earned her master's degree.

Keenan took his dinner into the living room and stretched out on the ancient couch, flipping through the channels before turning the television off and throwing the remote down on the coffee table. Nothing satisfied him anymore . . . not even TV.

Life would probably be easier if he moved out of this house. He could afford his own place, and there were advantages to living alone. But as much as it tortured him to live with Lucy, he couldn't imagine not seeing her every day. She'd be moving on in a year or so anyway. He could last that long.

Jessica came out of her room looking sleepy and tousled and sexy. Not for the first time, Keenan wondered why the hell he couldn't have a crush on *her*. They'd be great together. They both loved sex, and they both liked it a little rough. Jessica went through guys the way he went through girls, and she never had any hard feelings after a break-up.

Jessica was his kind of woman. They were perfect for each other.

They'd actually tried fooling around once. But in the middle of a kiss, they'd both cracked up. Only a few days later, realizing that their lack of sexual attraction to each other would make them perfect housemates, they'd found this place and talked Sami into sharing it with them. Jessica's friend Lucy had moved in a few weeks after that.

Jessica yawned. "Is that Sami's pizza?"

"Yeah."

She drifted into the kitchen and came back out with a slice. She shoved his feet off the couch and sat down, turning on the news. "Working at the club is screwing with my sleep cycle. Maybe it's time to quit. If the money weren't so good, I probably would. I'm getting too old for stripping."

"You're twenty-five."

"I feel fifty," she mumbled, her mouth full of pizza.

They sat in companionable silence for a few minutes, munching on their pizza slices and watching the news headlines crawl along the bottom of the screen. When the front door opened, they both looked up.

It was Lucy.

As always when he saw her, Keenan's pulse kicked into high gear. He started to look away, but then his gaze jerked back.

She looked different.

Her straight, shoulder-length blonde hair had been curled into ringlets. And her face . . .

She was wearing makeup, he realized with a sudden shock.

"What the hell happened to your face?" he demanded.

Jessica shot him a dirty look. "Nice, Diaz. Real nice." She looked back at Lucy with a smile. "You look great, Luce. What's up with the makeover?"

"I have a new job. Waitressing," she added. "I thought I'd get better tips if I did myself up a little."

"You vixen! You didn't say anything about getting a second job. You're not having money trouble, are you?"

Lucy shook her head. "No, but I thought a little extra income might come in handy." She sniffed the air. "Did Sami make pizza?"

"Yep."

"Great."

She disappeared into the kitchen, and Jessica leveled another glare at him. "What is wrong with you? You've been a total shit to Lucy this week."

He rubbed a hand across his eyes. "Yeah, I know."

Lucy came out with a slice of pizza and a bottle of water. "I've got some essays to grade, so I'm going to eat in my room. I'll see you later, okay?"

Her words appeared to be directed at Jessica, since she hadn't so much as glanced at him since she'd come in the door.

Jessica poked him in the ribs after Lucy was in her room. "You go in there and apologize for being a dick."

"I haven't been a dick," he said, even though he knew he had.

"Oh, please. The other night you said she was boring. It doesn't get much more dickish than that."

Keenan scowled down at the pizza crumbs on his plate. Jessica was right, but he couldn't tell her the real reason he acted like such an ass around Lucy.

But he had been worse than usual lately, and she deserved an apology.

"Fine," he said, taking his empty plate and beer bottle into the kitchen.

He stood at the back door for a moment, looking out at the Hawaiian night. Stars and a gibbous moon shown overhead, and the shadowy hump of Mount Tantalus made an inky patch to the west.

One of the many stupid things tourists said when they visited Hawaii was that the people who lived here must be happy all the time—as though living in a tropical paradise could inoculate you against trouble.

Of course that wasn't true. But Keenan was part Hawaiian—along with Japanese, Filipino, Irish and Hispanic—and even though looking at the valley his family had lived in for generations couldn't make all his pain go away, he did draw strength from it.

He took a deep breath, closed his eyes for a moment, and went to talk to Lucy.

* * *

As soon as she was in the privacy of her room, Lucy set her plate on the desk, dumped the contents of her backpack on the bed, and tried on one of the outfits Sheila had given her.

Over her navy blue lace thong, she wore a skin tight, see-through dress made of sheer mesh. The hem stopped at the top of her thighs, well above her navy blue garters. Her nipples were visible through it.

Everything was visible through it.

I have a good body, she thought.

No. She had a *great* body.

She wasn't used to thinking that about herself. But Sheila had said so, even though she'd also said Lucy had no idea how to use it.

"But the truth is, I'm desperate for new girls. The weekends are getting crazy busy and I need enough dancers to fill all three stages. You look cute even though you move like a piece of wood. If you promise to work on that, I'll put you on Friday and Saturday nights."

And Lucy found herself agreeing.

She thought back to her audition and couldn't help smiling. She'd gone out there in her pink satin bra and matching panties and the mini skirt she'd taken from the back of Jessica's closet. She was sweating like crazy and terrified she'd slip in her heels, even though it looked like she was wearing flats next to the other girls. That was probably one of the reasons she'd moved like a piece of wood.

But the men didn't seem to mind. One of the other dancers told her that the regulars knew Monday was audition night, and they liked to cheer on the "fresh meat".

And they had cheered for her. They'd whistled and catcalled and stuffed singles into the garter another dancer had lent her.

"Was it because I'm new?" she'd asked the dancer who'd lent her the garter. "Were they just being nice?"

The other dancer—Cinnamon, her stage name was—had laughed.

"Men in strip clubs aren't nice. They cheered because they like the way you look. You're going to do just fine here. But when Sheila gives you her notes, do what she says. She's been in this business a long time and she knows how to help a girl maximize her assets."

Sheila's "notes" had included giving her a few outfits to wear.

"They're twenty bucks apiece. The shoes are thirty-five. You can pay me out of your tips next week."

The shoes should have been terrifying—they were black patent leather platform pumps with five-inch heels—but Lucy, in spite of a lifetime wearing sneakers and flip flops and Birkenstocks, had fallen in love with them at first sight.

She adored the wicked gleam of the patent leather and the way they made her legs look a mile long. Slipping them on now, she took a couple of steps in front of the mirror.

It felt like she was on stilts, but she didn't fall. She tried a couple of hip thrusts.

Then, without warning, her bedroom door opened and Keenan stuck his head in.

"Lucy? Do you have a minute to—"

He froze, and so did she. Their eyes met in the mirror.

Then, as if he couldn't help himself, his eyes traveled down the length of her body.

She made a dive for the tee shirt she'd tossed over a chair, pulling it on over her head. "Get out!" she shouted through the material. "Get *out!*"

By the time her head poked through the neck hole, he was gone, the door closed behind him.

She pulled off her shoes with shaking hands. Her entire body felt flushed, as if her embarrassment were more than just her face could handle.

Oh God, oh God, oh God.

How could she ever face him again? He might as well have seen her naked.

She pulled on a pair of sweatpants and sat down on her bed, taking deep breaths to slow the agonized pounding of her heart.

The last thing she wanted to do was talk to him. But it was like getting back on a horse after you fell off. The longer you waited, the harder it would be.

She forced herself to leave the room, padding down the hallway in her bare feet to Keenan's bedroom door.

Before she could chicken out, she knocked.

"Yeah?" he called out, his voice sounding hesitant.

"It's me," she croaked out. She cleared her throat and tried again. "It's me, Keenan. Can I come in for a minute?"

There was a moment of silence. Then:

"Yeah."

She turned the knob and went in, closing the door behind her and leaning back against it.

Keenan was on his feet by his window, one of his hands gripping the sill behind him. She'd never seen him look so freaked out.

She'd also never seen him looking so gorgeous. Of course, she thought that every time she saw him.

He was wearing board shorts and no shirt, and his deeply tanned body was as flawless as an athlete's. His short black hair was the perfect frame for his high cheekbones and strong jaw, and his black eyes were like pools of India ink.

"Hey," she said, for lack of a better opening line.

"Hey."

A beat went by. She needed a second sentence. A second word, even.

But it was Keenan who broke the silence.

"What the hell kind of waitressing job did you get?"

She looked down at her feet. Her bare toes looked pale against the wood floors.

"Okay, so it's not exactly a waitressing job. It's more of a . . . dancing job."

"Holy shit. You're working in a *strip club?*"

He sounded outraged, which pissed her off.

"Why not?" she asked belligerently. "Jessica works at a strip club. You go to strip clubs. Why can't I work at one?"

"Because you—"

He stopped and looked away for a moment, running a hand through his dark hair.

"Because I what?" she asked.

He started to answer, but she cut him off. "No, let me guess. Because I'm not a risk-taker. Because I'm not exciting enough. Because I'm not sexy enough."

His jaw tightened. "Because you'll get eaten alive out there. Those places can be dangerous. Does Jessica know you're doing this?"

"No. And I don't want you to tell her. I'll tell her myself when I'm ready."

He scowled at her. "Which club are you working at?"

"Oh, right—like I'd tell you. The last thing I need is you coming down and making fun of me." She folded her arms. "And by the way . . . the men at the club didn't seem to find me as boring as you do."

He stared at her. "Please tell me you're not doing this because of all that stupid shit I said the other day. I was just yanking your chain, Lucy. You know I don't think you're boring."

She took a step closer to him. "It wasn't just that day. Last month when you read my thesis proposal, you told me I study life instead of living it."

He took a step closer to her. "I think what I actually said was that your thesis sounded fucking brilliant and that you should try to get it published."

This time she took two steps. "What you're conveniently forgetting is that you also said it's a good thing I have a career in academia ahead of me, since someone like me is better off living in an ivory tower than trying to cope with the real world."

His next step brought him within swinging distance, and Lucy had a sudden urge to slap that gorgeous face.

"Yeah, well, maybe I was right. Did you ever think about that, Lucy? That maybe you're too innocent to work in a fucking strip club? I mean, come on. You grew up in a small town in Vermont. Your parents are both professors. Your favorite way to spend Friday night is reading about cultural anthropology. What the hell do you think you're doing, traipsing down to a strip joint dressed in that—" He stopped suddenly and swallowed.

"Dressed in that . . . outfit."

Her cheeks burned, but she refused to give into her embarrassment. "Maybe I've decided to live life instead of reading about it, or listening to you and Jessica talk about it. Isn't that what you've been pushing me to do?"

"No! Not like this. You could get hurt, for Christ's sake. You think I want that?"

She took one more step, and now they were less than a foot apart. "I don't know what you want, Keenan. But I do know that the only person who's managed to hurt me lately is you."

She glared at him, and he glared at her.

Her heart was pounding. She was breathing hard, like she'd been running. Standing this close she could see the tension in Keenan's face—the way his dark brows had drawn together and the muscles along his jaw had hardened. His black eyes glittered. He looked angry and frustrated and pissed off.

And then, suddenly, something changed.

The electric sparks between them seemed to blur and shift. Their eyes locked, and Keenan's head bent towards her.

She froze for an instant. Then she she stumbled backwards until she felt the door at her back.

"What the hell are you doing?" she asked, her voice trembling.

"I..."

For a moment Keenan looked almost vulnerable. She couldn't read his expression. He took a step towards her, and she fumbled behind her for the doorknob.

When he saw that he stopped. And then, as if a shutter had closed, whatever emotion he'd been feeling was gone from his eyes.

"I'm not doing anything," he said coldly. "Did you think I was making a move on you, or something? Don't flatter yourself."

"Oh, I won't." This time when her voice trembled, it was with rage. "Don't you worry about that. I know the great Keenan Diaz would never be attracted to someone like me. But you know what I found out tonight? In spite of what you obviously think, I do have a wild side. A sexual side. And I'm looking forward to exploring it."

When she finally found the knob she yanked the door open, slipped through, and slammed it shut behind her.

She stomped down the hall and back to her bedroom, and this time when she closed the door she locked it, too.

CHAPTER 3

Keenan was in hell.

It was the Friday night after his confrontation with Lucy, and he was pacing back and forth in his bedroom, waiting for her to go to work.

This was all his fault. He'd driven her to this. He'd acted like a prick, and made Lucy feel bad about herself, and now she was stripping to prove she wasn't boring.

Fuck.

He'd kept an eye on her all week, determined to follow her to whatever club she was working at. When she didn't go anywhere on Tuesday or Wednesday or Thursday he started to hope that maybe she'd come to her senses and reconsidered her crazy plan. But that morning, when Jessica suggested going to a party that night, Lucy said she was busy.

He'd known immediately what she'd be busy doing.

What he should do was go to her room right now and talk to her. Beg her to forgive him. Even tell her the truth—that he'd only acted like an asshole because he was in love with her.

But on Monday night he'd gotten proof—as if he'd needed it—that she didn't feel the same way. In the grip of an attraction like nothing he'd ever felt, he'd started to kiss her. And she'd backed away from him like she was terrified . . . or maybe just horrified.

Horrified at the idea of kissing him.

Which she should be. When he thought of all the women he'd been with . . . and all the things he'd done with them . . . he knew he didn't belong within a hundred miles of a sweet girl like Lucy.

And she was only in Hawaii to get her degree. Even if she wanted to be with him—and she'd made it very clear that she didn't—a relationship between them would only be temporary.

He'd never tell her how he felt. But that didn't mean he wouldn't protect her. It was his fault she was pulling this crazy stripper shit, and he was going to do whatever it took to make sure she was safe.

Of course he knew Lucy well enough to know he had to be smart about it. He couldn't go all alpha on her and drag her away from the club.

As he knew from playing video games with her, any hint that someone was trying to overpower her would bring out the she-demon within. Lucy might be innocent when it came to men but she was fiercely independent and stubborn as hell, and she'd never put up with him ordering her around.

So he'd have to figure something else out. His family had lived in Hawaii forever and he knew a lot of people. He might know someone who worked at her club.

So the first step was finding out which club it was.

A door closed down the hall. He stopped pacing and listened.

Jessica and Sami were out for the night, so it had to be Lucy.

She paused outside his door, and he held his breath. She hadn't spoken to him all week. Maybe she'd knock on his door, ask to talk, and they could actually have a rational conversation about this.

But after a moment her footsteps continued down the hall. Then he heard the front door close.

He expelled the breath he'd been holding. Okay, so rationality wasn't an option. Which meant he was back to his original plan: pretending to be James Bond.

It was after sunset, and he'd already put on dark clothes. Now he slipped out the back door and waited in the shadows for Lucy to back out of the garage. Once she was headed down the street, he climbed on his bike and went after her.

* * *

Okay, so now he knew which club Lucy was working at. *Centerfolds* in Waikiki.

The good news was it was a no-touching club. Lucy wouldn't be giving lap dances. And if a customer put a finger on her—other than to slide money into her garter—he'd be thrown out on his ass.

The bad news was he didn't know anyone who worked here.

She'd been inside about ten minutes. Was that enough time for her to get changed and put her makeup on and go up on stage?

It was time to get in there.

He paid his cover charge—twenty bucks, which included two drinks—and headed up the stairs.

He might not know this particular club but he knew strip clubs in general, and he knew there'd be a place for him to skulk in the shadows. Even if Lucy happened to glance his way, she probably wouldn't recognize him in his dark clothes and the baseball cap he'd borrowed from Sami.

In any case, he was willing to risk it. He was willing to risk anything to make sure Lucy didn't get herself into a bad situation.

As soon as he went through the door he saw he'd been right about the dark corners. He found a seat off to the side that was almost entirely in shadow, and scanned the three stages quickly to see if Lucy was on one of them.

She wasn't, but his relief was short-lived. The set ended and the dancers changed stages, with the group on the stage nearest him exiting towards the dressing room and a new group of dancers coming out of the dressing room and onto the stage furthest from him.

Lucy was in that group.

His body had never been such a battlefield of conflicting emotions. Shock and confusion and a wave of lust that hit like a tsunami—and a primitive instinct of protectiveness that demanded he go up on that stage, throw Lucy over his shoulder, and get her away from the hungry eyes of the men watching her.

She was wearing the outfit he'd gotten a glimpse of the other night. He'd re-imagined that moment so many times he'd started to think it couldn't have been as hot as it was in his head.

It was.

Under the stage lights, Lucy's skin was creamy and flawless. Her curves were delicate rather than bodacious, but to Keenan they seemed just right. Her breasts were small but exquisite, her rosy nipples clearly visible under her see-through dress, and when she turned around . . . Christ. Her ass was fucking perfect.

She'd left her hair straight tonight, and it looked soft and touchable as she swished it around. Her makeup made her lips even fuller and her blue eyes even bigger.

But what made her stand out among the more experienced, polished dancers around her was a kind of glow she radiated—a glow of innocence, enthusiasm, and sheer enjoyment.

Lucy was having a ball.

It was the last thing Keenan had expected. When he'd pictured Lucy dancing at a strip club, he'd imagined her doing it with a kind of grim determination—the same expression she wore when they played each other at chess or *Assassin's Creed.* He'd assumed that this whole gig was about proving him wrong . . . proving, like she'd said that night, that she did have a wild, sexual side.

And maybe that was part of it. But Keenan realized, now, that what he'd unconsciously been assuming was dead wrong. He'd thought that Lucy on stage would look like a girl trying to prove something that wasn't true—trying to be something she wasn't. He'd thought she'd look like a girl *pretending* to have a wild, sexual side.

Instead, she looked like a girl letting that part of herself out for the first time. A part of herself that had always been there, just below the surface.

He couldn't take his eyes off her.

She might not be an experienced stripper, but he should have remembered that she was a trained dancer.

Her moves weren't as calculated and practiced as those of the other strippers, but she had natural grace. The combination of that grace with her sweet, shy, sexy vibe made her irresistible.

He followed her every move in a kind of trance. He could never get enough of watching her, of letting his eyes rove over her slender curves and soft skin. And when she shook that sweet, firm, perfect ass . . .

A wave of hunger, dark and powerful, shook him to the core. His cock hardened. His hands twitched.

And then a wolf whistle from one of the men sitting at the stage sent another emotion coursing through him.

Rage.

Every cell in his body screamed that Lucy was his—that no other man had the right to see her like this. No other man could lust after her the way he was lusting after her.

He got to his feet before he realized what he was doing. But before he could do something crazy—something Lucy would never forgive him for—a group of guys came into the club, talking and laughing.

He knew two of those guys. They'd gone to the same high school, and they still surfed together once in a while.

If they recognized him, they'd probably call him by name. And Lucy might find out he was here.

He tipped his baseball cap a little lower and retreated deeper into the shadows. Once the guys had settled themselves at one of the stages, he slipped out the door and down the stairs. A minute later he was outside the club.

His drink tickets were still in his pocket.

* * *

The ride back home was mostly uphill, which seemed appropriate. He'd coasted down to Waikiki fueled by urgency and determination, and now he was forcing his mind and body to put what he'd seen behind him.

He had no right, none at all, to interfere in Lucy's life. He might have had some excuse if she'd seemed miserable up there or even conflicted . . . but she hadn't.

She'd seemed happy.

What kind of asshole was he that Lucy's happiness made him want to punch someone?

He'd always known she'd leave eventually—a girl that smart and focused had a big academic career ahead of her in some fancy Ivy League college. She'd never settle down in Hawaii. There wasn't enough here for her.

But seeing her up on that stage made him feel like she'd left him in a way he hadn't been expecting . . . or prepared for.

He punished himself on the last hill, trying to ease the ache in his heart with physical effort. By the time he parked his bike and went inside the house, he was covered in a sheen of sweat but didn't feel any better.

Sami and Jessica weren't home yet, and probably wouldn't be for a while. He had the house to himself.

He stripped off his sweaty clothes, turned on the shower, and made the water as hot as he could stand. Then he stood under the spray with his head bent and his eyes closed, trying to figure out how to handle what was happening inside him.

He'd embarrassed Lucy a lot the last few months, needling her about her sexual naïveté and her lack of interest in dating since Bug Guy. But he realized now that her single status had been the only thing keeping him sane while they lived under the same roof. Maybe he was the wrong man for her, maybe she didn't have feelings for him, but at least no one else had what he couldn't have.

Now he could no longer pretend Lucy belonged to him in any way, shape, or form. She'd taken charge of her sexuality the way she'd taken charge of her academic career, and the result was more than he could handle.

After at least twenty minutes under the hot water, he turned off the faucet and toweled himself off. He was going to have to move out after all. He wouldn't get his engineering master's for another few months but he already had a job lined up, and he made plenty of money on the weekends bartending. He could afford his own place.

And there was no way in hell he could go on living here.

CHAPTER 4

Lucy couldn't stop smiling as she drove home at two o'clock in the morning. She should have felt exhausted after six hours of dancing, but instead she felt energized.

Not to mention rich.

She'd made four hundred dollars that night. *Four hundred dollars.*

A girl could pay off her student loans moonlighting as a stripper.

One of the girls told her that you could make even better money at a lap dance club, if you could handle it. And while Lucy knew her current mood of experimentation probably wouldn't carry her that far, she found herself fantasizing about giving a lap dance . . . to one particular man.

After Lucy got home and turned off the engine, she sat for a while in the silent car, letting her head fall back and her eyes close.

"Did you think I was making a move on you? Don't flatter yourself."

If she gave Keenan a lap dance, she could make him eat those words. She could make him want her.

In her fantasies, anyway.

Lucy sighed and forced herself back to reality. The house was dark and silent, so she let herself in as quietly as possible and kicked off her shoes, padding down the hallway towards her bedroom in bare feet.

She paused for a moment as she passed Keenan's room. She wondered how many times she'd stood outside his door like this, wishing she had the courage to just walk in there, take off her clothes, and crawl into his bed naked.

He'd made it clear the other night that he wasn't attracted to her, but maybe if he were half-asleep and a naked woman pressed herself against him, his instincts would take over and he'd make love to her before he realized what was happening. Keenan was so sexual . . . he'd made that clear enough in the stories he told.

Thoughts of his exploits depressed her again. He always told his stories as crudely as possible, and it seemed almost pointed—as though he were trying to emphasize the fact that someone like her could never be enough for someone like him in the bedroom.

"Lucy."

She froze. It was Keenan's voice, coming from behind his closed door. How could he know she was out here?

"Lucy..."

What the hell? Did he want her to come in?

Confused, uncertain, Lucy turned the knob silently and peered into the dark room.

It took a moment for her eyes to adjust. But moonlight shone in through the window, softly illuminating Keenan's sleeping form, and it wasn't long before she could see him clearly.

He *was* asleep. He was on his back, his arms flung out to the sides. A sheet covered him up to his waist, so she couldn't tell if he was wearing boxers or pajama bottoms or anything at all, but his torso was definitely bare.

And beautiful.

But she couldn't stand here and ogle him. He was asleep, which meant she must've imagined hearing her name. Or maybe he'd muttered something in his sleep that had sounded like—

"Lucy."

Her heart thumped. Shit, shit, shit. Had he woken up?

She stood poised for flight, but then she took another look at his face.

His eyes were closed. He was still asleep.

Which meant . . . which meant . . .

Keenan shifted restlessly in his sleep, and the sheet pulled a little tighter across his hips.

That was when she saw it.

His erection.

Keenan had an erection, and he was saying her name in his sleep.

"Lucy . . ." he said again, his voice a seductive whisper. And then, a groan: "*Lucy.*"

For one more moment she just stood there. Then she backed out of the room, closed the door silently behind her, and fled down the hall.

Safe in her own room, Lucy went over to the window and pressed her forehead against the glass. Her heart was pounding and she was trembling all over. She took a deep breath and then another.

Calm down, she told herself.

She forced herself to change into pajamas and get into bed, even though she knew sleep would be impossible.

She had to think this through.

Keenan had called out her name in his sleep . . . not once but several times. And the tone of his voice had been sexy. Lustful, even.

And he'd been hard.

Dreaming of her made him hard.

It was almost impossible to believe. She'd fantasized so many times about Keenan wanting her that way that she could hardly wrap her mind around what she'd seen.

Keenan hard . . . because of *her*.

Had his feelings changed after he saw her stripper outfit last week? No—that didn't make sense. They'd fought after that, and he'd told her not to flatter herself that he would ever make a move on her.

Suddenly she sat straight up in bed, bending her knees to her chest and wrapping her arms around her shins. Maybe when they were having that fight . . . maybe he really *had* been about to kiss her.

But why would he lie about it? If he really did want her that way, why wouldn't he say so? He wasn't exactly shy about propositioning women.

Except for friends. He never crossed the line with Jessica. Maybe he had a rule about housemates being off-limits, or something.

And there was his whole no-relationship rule. He'd always made it clear that sex, for him, was about scratching an itch and getting his ya-yas out. It was never about anything deeper. It was always temporary.

Maybe that was why he didn't have sex with women he considered friends. Because you couldn't just ditch a friend after you slept together. Not unless you were willing to lose the friendship. And based on a year of living with him, of seeing him with Jessica and Sami, Lucy knew that Keenan's friends were important to him.

And even though they tangled with each other a lot, she knew that she and Keenan were friends, too.

But these feelings she had for him weren't going to go away. And now that she knew he felt something for her, too...

She rolled over onto her stomach and buried her face in her pillow. What should she do? What should she *do*?

She rolled onto her back again and took a deep breath. She wasn't going to figure it all out tonight. She needed to try to get some sleep so she could— hopefully—think clearly in the morning. Or at least more clearly than she was thinking right now.

"Lucy..."

The memory of Keenan's voice saying her name sent a wave of heat through her. Her eyes drifted closed and her hand drifted downward, ghosting over the triangle between her legs.

"Keenan . . ." she whispered, as she stroked herself through her pajamas.

God, she wanted him.

And now she knew he wanted her, too.

* * *

Lucy didn't get much sleep that night. She woke bleary-eyed and muddle-headed, and made her way towards the kitchen like a homing pigeon in search of coffee.

Keenan and Jessica and Sami were already there, sitting around the table having breakfast.

"Lucy! Maybe you can talk Keenan out of this," Sami said, pouring coffee for her into the blue mug she always used.

"Talk him out of what?" Lucy said cautiously, sitting down in her usual chair and taking a grateful sip of the hot, rich brew. She glanced at Keenan but he wasn't looking at her. He was scowling down at his plate, his jaw tight and the fingers of his right hand drumming on the table.

"He's moving out," Jessica said.

For a few seconds she stopped breathing. If it weren't a physical impossibility she would have said her heart stopped beating.

In that frozen moment of time, Keenan looked up and met her eyes. He looked away again almost immediately, but in that instant Lucy had seen pain and confusion and a kind of baffled anger.

"Well," she said slowly, "if Keenan wants to move out I guess there's nothing we can do about it." She paused. "Why now, though? If you don't mind my asking."

He shrugged, his gaze focused on the view through the kitchen window. A rainbow arched over the mountains to the west.

"It just seemed like the right time. I'm graduating soon and starting my job at Morgan Engineering. Of course I'll pay my share of the rent until you find a new housemate."

Jessica and Sami both started talking, but Lucy didn't hear them. She was staring at Keenan's profile and wondering.

Could Keenan be leaving because of her? Because he was attracted to her and, for some reason, didn't want to be?

Twenty-four hours ago, the idea would have been unthinkable. And yet . . .

Keenan glanced at the kitchen clock. "We can talk more about this tonight, okay? I want to get to the gym."

And without another word he got up from the table and left. A minute later they saw him on his bike, heading down the street with his broad shoulders hunched over and his head down.

"Well," Jessica said, folding her arms. "How do you like that?"

Lucy took a deep breath. "Jessica, would you mind if I talk to you in private for a minute? I have a big favor to ask you."

* * *

Keenan stayed out of the house all day.

He went to the gym and worked out like a demon. He hiked the Manoa Falls trail and stood in the pool at the base of the waterfall, letting the cataracts of water flow over him. He went to his favorite beach and swam for hours, waiting for the peace the ocean always brought him.

It didn't come.

He lay on the warm sand and let the sun's heat soak into his bones, but that didn't soothe the turmoil inside him, either.

Finally, after sunset, he made his way back home. He figured Lucy would have gone to the club by now, so he wouldn't risk seeing her.

But as he came up the street towards the little white house he'd lived in for the last year, he saw Lucy sitting on the front steps.

He stopped, but she'd already spotted him. It was too late to turn around and pretend he'd never been here.

He pedaled the rest of the way and parked his bike in the garage as usual. Then he hesitated. Should he go in through the back door and avoid Lucy, or go around to the front and say hi?

The question was answered for him.

"Hey," Lucy said, and he turned to see her standing in the garage doorway, smiling at him.

She was wearing an outfit he'd never seen before. It was a blue slip dress the color of her eyes, form-fitting and silky and with a hemline that barely reached mid-thigh.

A bolt of lust went straight to his groin, and he reacted the way he usually did when that happened.

By being an asshole.

"What are you so dressed up for?" he growled.

They had a tried-and-true pattern for moments like this. Lucy would respond to his bad temper with a snarl of her own, which would usually lead to a pointless argument, grumpy apologies, and, finally, a game of *Call of Duty* or *Assassin's Creed* with the loser making popcorn.

He realized suddenly how much he would miss those nights with Lucy, sitting close together on the beat up old couch as they manipulated their avatars, trash-talking each other with abandon and fighting over the last handful of popcorn.

But Lucy didn't follow their usual pattern.

"I'm dressed up because I'm taking you out for a drink."

He and Lucy had spent plenty of time together over the last year, but they'd never gone out for a drink. Not just the two of them, anyway.

God, he wanted to. He wanted to sit across from Lucy at a little table in a dark bar and pretend she was his.

"Why do you want to do that?"

She shrugged. "Lots of reasons. To congratulate you on your job offer from Morgan. To congratulate you on your 3.8 G.P.A. last semester. To say goodbye . . . since you'll be moving out soon."

He slid his hands into the pockets of his shorts. "You're not mad that I'm going? Like Sami and Jessica are?"

"Why should I be? It's your life. You should live where you want to live."

So she didn't really care that he was leaving. His heart felt strangely heavy.

"Yeah. Well. You'll be moving out too, right? Once you finish your thesis and get your degree."

Lucy looked at him thoughtfully. "Is that what you think? That I'll be leaving Hawaii?"

"Well, yeah. You don't really belong here, do you? You've got a big academic career ahead of you. You'll probably be tenured at some fancy college before you're thirty-five."

She smiled. "I'm not thinking that far ahead, to be honest. And I'm not graduating for another year. A lot can happen in a year. So do you want to come out with me, or not?"

Yes.

His hands tightened into fists. "Don't you have to work at the club tonight?"

"Nope. I told them I needed tonight off. Of course if you've got other plans, I guess I could call and ask them to put me back on the schedule."

Maybe he couldn't stop her from stripping forever, but he could at least stop her from stripping tonight.

"No," he said quickly. "A drink sounds good. Just give me a few minutes to change, okay?"

"Sure."

It didn't take him long. He took a quick shower and then, after a moment's hesitation, put on a pair of khakis and a dark gray polo shirt. He might as well do Lucy's outfit justice.

Her eyebrows went up when she saw him. "You look great," she said.

"Thanks." He realized belatedly that he hadn't said anything about how she looked. "That dress is . . . nice." *Weak, Diaz.* "It's beautiful, actually. Is it new?"

She nodded. "Jessica and I went shopping today." She smiled at him. "Since I'm taking you out, will you let me drive?"

He hesitated. If it had been Jessica, he would have said yes. But with Lucy, something inside him insisted that he should be the one to drive—even though this wasn't a date.

"How about I drive? That way you won't have to worry about what you're drinking."

"But I don't want you to worry, either."

"I weigh a hell of a lot more than you do. A couple of drinks won't even faze me."

She tilted her head as she looked up at him. "I guess you are a little bigger than I am." She reached for his hand and put hers against it, palm to palm. "Okay, a lot bigger."

He stared down at their hands for a moment, mesmerized. Lucy was so small, so delicate. He was almost a foot taller than she was, and at least a hundred pounds heavier.

A surge of protectiveness went through him. Before he could stop himself, he closed his hand around her much smaller one.

Shit.

He dropped her hand quickly and cleared his throat. "So where do you want to go?"

She led the way to his car, which he kept parked on the street. "I thought Anna Bee's. If that's okay?"

"Sure." Anna Bee's was in downtown Honolulu, frequented more by locals than tourists. It had comfortable booths and low lighting, and the thought of sitting across from Lucy at one of those candlelit tables made his skin feel hot and tight.

Without thinking he went around to the passenger side and opened Lucy's door for her.

"Thanks," she said, looking surprised.

Damn. He had to be more careful, or he'd do or say something that made it painfully clear how he felt about her.

This isn't a date, he reminded himself as he went around to the driver's side.

No matter how much he wished it could be.

CHAPTER 5

"You know, I don't think you ever told me why you went into engineering," Lucy said as the waiter brought over their drinks. Keenan had beer and she'd ordered a Long Island iced tea, knowing she would need a lot of liquid courage to go through with her plan for tonight.

"What do you mean?" Keenan asked before taking a swig from the bottle.

"Well . . . your dad's an investment banker, right? And your mom's a financial advisor?"

"Yeah."

"So did you ever think about going into finance or stock broking or whatever?"

Keenan seemed to relax a little as he thought about her question, which was one of the reasons she'd asked it. Lull him into a false sense of security and then go in for the kill.

There was another reason, too. Before she took a step that would change things between them forever—no matter what the result—she wanted to have a real conversation with Keenan. Just the two of them talking, without the buffer of video games or a chess board or their housemates, and without the snark and defensiveness and needling that always seemed to color their interactions.

"I guess so, yeah. I was always pretty good at math, and with money, too. I got my first job and my first bank account when I was sixteen, and as soon as I was old enough—and got a job that offered one—I started contributing to a 401k."

"You did?" Lucy had always thought of herself as more grownup than Keenan, because he spent so much time surfing and partying. But to her, a 401k was still something that belonged to the future. Maybe there were different ways to think about being adult.

"Yeah. But when it came time for college, my parents both said I should study something I love. And when I thought about it, I realized I don't love money or finance or the stock market. I love making things, you know? Physical things. Things real people will use. Things that will make the world a better place."

She rested her cheek on her hand as she looked at him. "That's cool," she said seriously. "Is that why you took the job with Morgan? They make medical devices, right?"

He nodded. "Yeah. My grandfather had an operation a few years ago, and a new kind of medical endoscope basically saved his life. I started reading articles about it, and for a high school science project I interviewed the mechanical engineer who designed the device. That's when I decided to study engineering."

He took another swig of beer, and Lucy took a sip of her drink.

"What about you?" Keenan asked as he set his bottle back on the table. "How did you get into anthropology?"

She grinned at him. "According to you, I got into anthropology because I'd rather study life than live it."

Keenan winced. "That was a shitty thing to say. I'm sorry about that."

She shrugged. "It's okay. It's not the whole truth, but it is part of the truth. I mean, I am more comfortable observing than participating. But I also really love anthropology. Especially dance ethnography. I love studying the way dance reflects culture and society. Like hula here in Hawaii."

He nodded. "I liked your thesis proposal about hula and language. I'm part Hawaiian, but I didn't know . . . or maybe I forgot . . . that the ancient Hawaiians never developed a written language. And I thought your theory was really cool—that for them, music and dance embodied language in a way that made writing unnecessary."

Lucy felt a warm rush of pleasure. "You remember that?"

"Well, yeah. I just read it last month." He hesitated. "I never told you this, but I actually used to dance hula."

"You did?"

He nodded. "My great-aunt had a halau."

"A hula school?"

"Yeah. All the kids in our family studied with her."

"Why didn't you ever tell me that? You know I'm researching hula."

He shrugged. "I don't usually tell mainlanders I'm a trained dancer. Especially mainland girls," he added with a grin. "It doesn't fit into their image of me as a he-man."

"Well, then, they're idiots. The sexiest thing I ever saw in my life was a group of men performing a hula kahiko—an ancient dance."

"You thought that was sexy?"

She kept her eyes on his. "Absolutely."

For a moment they just looked at each other. In the low, intimate lighting of Anna Bee's, Keenan's eyes were black as pitch.

A girl could get lost in those eyes.

Keenan cleared his throat and looked away. "You want another drink?"

"Sure," she said, even though she hadn't finished her first one.

She'd better stop after two, though. Being a little tipsy would help her with her plan, but being drunk off her ass was probably a bad idea.

A wave of nervousness made her skin tingle. Could she really go through with what she had in mind?

At that moment, a girl walked past their table, paused, and came back towards them. "Keenan," she said. "I thought that was you. How've you been?"

Keenan looked up. "Hey, Leilani. I'm good. You?"

"Good." She paused. "My door is still open, by the way." She grinned. "My bedroom door, that is."

Keenan looked uncomfortable. "Okay, well, see you around."

The girl nodded, sent an interested glance in Lucy's direction, and continued on her way.

Keenan frowned down at the table, avoiding her eyes. That was a relief, in a way, because Lucy was terrified her reaction was showing in her face.

And that reaction was jealousy.

Pure, primitive, cavewoman jealousy.

Keenan never brought his dates home, which meant she never met them. And of course he didn't bring his girlfriends home, because Keenan didn't have girlfriends.

It turned out that that was a damn good thing. Because when Lucy was confronted with one of the girls Keenan had slept with, she had to fight the urge to leap over the table and claw her eyes out.

So could she go through with her plan for tonight?

Hell, yes.

* * *

Keenan stopped at two beers, because he was driving and Lucy would be in the car. But even though he took his time with the second one, he wasn't ready for the evening to end by the time he finished it.

He was about to suggest getting some food somewhere, even though Lucy had already eaten dinner, when she smiled across the table at him.

"Do you feel like taking a walk? I have a favor to ask you."

"Sure," he said, relief spreading through him at the knowledge that he didn't have to take her home just yet.

It was only after they'd settled their bill—he'd solved the problem of who would pay by giving his credit card to the waiter when Lucy was in the restroom—and had left Anna Bee's that he remembered Lucy had mentioned a favor.

"You said you had something to ask me," he reminded her as they strolled down the city sidewalk.

She nodded. "Yes. I wondered if you . . ." She paused and stopped walking.

Keenan stopped, too, and realized they were in front of *Sweet Bliss*—the club Jessica worked at.

"Do you mind if we stop in here for a second?" Lucy asked. "I need to ask Jessica something."

He felt a little weird about going into a strip club with Lucy, especially if Jessica was inside. He'd stopped coming to this club once she started working here.

"Well . . ."

"It'll just take a minute. I told her we might stop by tonight, and she's cool with it."

He sighed. "Okay." If Jessica was on stage or giving a lap dance, he'd just make sure he was looking someplace else.

This club had no cover charge and no doorman, although there were bouncers inside. There was only one stage, off to the side, while the rest of the club was set up for lap dances—semi-dark recesses where a guy could sit alone, and larger tables where bachelor parties and other groups could gather.

Sweet Bliss was a popular club, and even though it was still early it was fairly crowded. Lucy looked around, spotted an empty recess, and steered Keenan over to it. "Jess is probably backstage. Wait here for me, okay?"

Before he could answer, she was gone.

Keenan sighed and sat in the worn leather armchair. It was tucked away in a dark nook, designed for those customers who wanted privacy while they were turned on.

Being a normal red-blooded male, Keenan usually enjoyed strip clubs. But tonight, out with Lucy, he had no desire to look at any other woman. He leaned back, folded his arms, and closed his eyes.

Five minutes later he heard Lucy's voice again.

"Hey there."

He opened his eyes, and his jaw dropped.

Lucy had changed out of the blue slip dress into the sexiest lingerie he'd ever seen. She was wearing a black lace bra and matching thong, along with a black lace garter belt and thigh-high fishnets. A pair of black spike heels completed the outfit.

As long as he lived, he'd never want a woman the way he wanted Lucy Barnaby. Beside her, every other woman seemed to fade into black and white, leaving Lucy in vibrant, burnished, soul-searing color.

"What the fuck," he growled. He tried to look away, but he couldn't. His eyes travelled down her body and back up to her face.

She was smiling.

"You remember I had a favor to ask you?"

"Yeah," he grated, keeping his eyes on hers with an effort.

"Well . . . I decided not to take the job at *Centerfolds*."

His heart sank to his toes. "You mean—you're going to work here, instead?"

There was no way in hell he could handle that. The idea of Lucy giving lap dances to strange men made him want to kill someone.

But she shook her head. "No, I'm not going to work here either. This whole stripper thing was just something I needed to try. To prove that I could. To let that part of myself out. You know?"

He was having a hard time focusing on what she was saying. How the hell was he supposed to think straight with Lucy standing there dressed like that?

"Yeah," he said, hoping it was the right response.

"So now that I've done it, I don't really need to do it anymore. Except . . . there's still one thing I haven't done that I want to do. And you're the perfect person to help me with that."

What the hell did she need help with that involved her wearing a garter belt—and not much else?

"Uh . . ."

Lucy took a few steps closer and leaned forward, putting her hands on the arms of his chair.

Lust and adrenaline prickled his skin.

"I want to give a lap dance. Just to experience what it's like. I don't want to give one to a stranger, but I don't want to give one to a guy I know who might get the wrong idea, either. So . . ."

Her eyes searched his. "I know you, and I trust you, but you've made it clear that you're not attracted to me. So you're perfect. I asked Jess if the club owner would let me do it here, and she said no problem. And since she isn't actually working tonight, we don't have to worry about her seeing us, which would be weird."

She leaned a little closer, and he got a faint whiff of perfume. It was the scent she wore on special occasions—Opium by Yves Saint Laurent.

"So what do you say?" she whispered. "Will you let me experiment on you?"

Maybe if he had all his faculties, he could've figured a way out of it. But he didn't have all his faculties. He was half out of his mind with desire, his cock already hard with it. He had three functioning brain cells at the moment . . . if he was lucky.

He tried to think.

If he said no, she'd find someone else to experiment on. He couldn't let that happen.

But if he said yes . . .

"You should know . . ." His voice came out as a croak, and he cleared his throat. "If we do this, I want you to understand that I'll probably . . . react. That's just biology. It doesn't mean anything."

Lucy nodded. "I know. That's why you're perfect." She smiled at him. "So . . . is that a yes?"

He didn't trust his voice, so he just nodded.

"Perfect timing," Lucy said, as the song playing through the speakers ended and another began.

It was by the Black Keys, one of his favorite bands. There was a blues beat behind their songs that he loved—and that was sexy as hell.

Lucy slid her hands up the chair arms until her face was inches from his and the tips of her breasts just brushed against his shirt.

"You know the rules, right?" she said softly. "I'm allowed to touch you, but you can't touch me. You have to stay still."

He nodded again. He'd gotten lap dances before, though not lately, and he'd never had trouble following the rules. But now he had an overwhelming urge to grip Lucy's hips and put his mouth on her breast.

Hell, he had an urge to unzip his pants, shove her thong to the side, and fuck her right here on the chair.

But he could control himself. He had to. Because then Lucy would be finished with her stripper experiment, and he wouldn't have to make himself sick worrying about her.

Keeping her safe was worth any price he had to pay.

Even if that price was his sanity.

CHAPTER 6

Maybe it was the Long Island iced tea buzzing through her veins. Maybe it was the music, which she'd paid the DJ twenty bucks to play.

Whatever the reason, Lucy felt confident and sexy in a way she never had before.

Maybe it was because Keenan, for almost the first time since she'd known him, didn't look confident at all.

He was a man who preferred to be in charge when it came to relationships. He set the boundaries; he set the terms. And in his stories about his sex life, he'd made it clear that he liked to be in charge in the bedroom, too.

Lucy had always thought he'd regaled them with his exploits in a deliberate effort to embarrass her. But since she'd heard him murmur her name in his sleep, she'd wondered if there might be another reason.

To scare her off.

Well, he hadn't scared her off. He'd made her braver. Because she wanted Keenan Diaz, and she was willing to take risks to get him.

Including dressing in black lace underwear and giving him a lap dance.

She'd never done anything like this in her life, and she should have been nervous as hell. Instead she felt excited—and powerful.

"I wonder what I should do first?" she murmured. "This is my first time, after all. Do you have any suggestions?"

His mouth opened, but no sound came out for a moment.

"I . . . don't know," he said finally. His voice was hoarse.

"Then I guess I'll just have to figure it out for myself."

Jessica had said she could be topless for a lap dance but that her g-string had to stay on. Lucy took her hands off Keenan's chair and backed up a few steps, keeping her eyes on his as she reached around to unhook her bra. Then she let it slip down her arms and onto the floor.

The club was air-conditioned, and Lucy wasn't sure if it was that or the way Keenan's eyes dropped to her breasts that made her nipples pucker and tighten.

She watched the flare of his nostrils and the jump of his throat muscles as he swallowed. Then she came close again, leaned forward, and put her hands on Keenan's shoulders.

She'd meant to press her breasts against his chest, but his legs were in her way. So she backed up again, put her hands on his knees, and exerted steady pressure until he let his legs open in a V. Then she moved into the space she'd created and leaned into him.

He was *hard.*

She darted a glance at his face, but his eyes were closed. His lips were pressed together and his dark brows were drawn together in a fierce scowl.

Keenan had told her it would just be biology if his body reacted, but she didn't believe that.

He was hard because he wanted her.

The knowledge should have spurred her on, but suddenly she felt like an actress who'd forgotten her lines. What the hell was she supposed to do now?

Jessica had showed her a YouTube video of a lap dance. She replayed the video in her head, took a deep breath, and slid her arms around Keenan's neck.

That brought her body flush against his. Her naked breasts were pressed against his chest.

She could feel his heart pounding.

Somehow, that affected her even more than his erection had. Finding her courage again she began to move, slowly, getting the feel of what she was doing. She shifted so she was straddling his right thigh and could rub her leg against the thick ridge of his arousal.

She heard the sharp intake of his breath.

She found herself undulating against him, letting the music flow through her. She felt like a siren, a temptress, a sex goddess.

His whole body tensed beneath hers. His breath grew ragged.

Then she turned around and settled against him in the classic lap dance position—her butt against his crotch.

An electric bolt of excitement made her skin tingle. His erection was pushing against her ass, and the sensation sent a rush of heat from her nipples to her clit.

She let go completely then, arching her back and letting her head rest against his shoulder as she moved against him, rubbing harder and faster with the driving beat of the music.

She could hear Keenan panting now, as though he were running a race. His body was hard as a rock behind her—his chest, his abs, his thighs, his cock.

Her own body grew soft and pliant in response. She realized with a shock that her g-string was soaked with her arousal, but she didn't feel embarrassed.

Behind her, Keenan growled.

Something about that sound seared through her. She had a crazy desire to lie down on the floor in front of him and spread her legs, begging him to take her right there in the club. The urge was so powerful she was almost relieved when the song ended.

She took a moment to calm herself, taking a long, deep breath before pushing to her feet and turning to face Keenan again.

It was a good thing she'd taken that breath, because when she saw Keenan's face her lungs stopped working.

His black eyes were wild, his lips drawn back in a snarl. He looked like a chained animal one snapped link away from leaping on her and devouring her whole.

A tremor went through her, but it wasn't fear.

She picked up her bra from the floor and took her time putting it back on. Once it was in place, she met Keenan's eyes.

"There's something I need you to know," she said. "Whenever you talked about your sexual relationships, you thought I turned red and left the room because I was embarrassed. You thought that when you talked about tying women down and dominating them I was freaked out or grossed out or turned off."

Heat rose in her cheeks but she continued to look him straight in the eyes. "You were wrong. When I turned red and left the room it wasn't because I was turned off. It was because I was turned on. I was turned on, and I didn't know how to deal with it, and I was afraid you'd find out."

She backed up a few steps. "I'm going to change now. If you're still here when I come back, we can drive home together." She paused. "By the way . . . Jessica and Sami are going to a party tonight and they're planning to stay over. We'll have the house to ourselves."

Then she turned and walked away.

She barely noticed the dancers and customers she passed on her way to the dressing room. Her legs felt shaky and she was trembling all over.

She'd put everything on the line. She'd literally put herself out there, and the next move was up to Keenan.

Would he still be there when she got back?

She thought he would.

She put her shoes and lingerie in Jessica's locker and pulled on her sandals and slip dress. She checked her face in the mirror, took a deep breath, and went back out into the club.

A dancer stopped her as she passed the bar. "Are you Lucy Barnaby?"

When Lucy said yes she handed her a set of car keys. "Keenan left these for you. He said he's not going home tonight but he'll see you tomorrow."

Lucy's hand closed around the keys automatically and she thanked the girl. Then, feeling numb, she left the club and headed towards the parking lot where Keenan had left his car.

Rejected. She'd been completely and totally rejected.

God, what an idiot she was. Here she'd been feeling all sexy and thinking Keenan wanted her, when what he'd said was the exact truth. If his body had reacted to her lap dance, it was only because he was a guy and that was biology.

Who the hell knew why he'd said her name in his sleep. Maybe he had sex dreams about every woman he knew.

And considering all the women who passed in and out of his life, there was a good chance he knew more than one Lucy. Maybe he'd been dreaming about some other girl.

She unlocked Keenan's car and sat in the driver's seat, staring through the windshield but not seeing anything. She'd never felt so humiliated in her life. The image of what she must have looked like giving that lap dance flashed before her, and she cringed.

Rubbing against him like a cat in heat . . . wriggling her butt against his crotch . . . pressing her naked breasts against his chest.

And the whole time he'd been thinking . . . what?

He'd been turned on, but that was because he was a guy and she was half-naked.

He must have been mortified. Or worse—sorry for her.

She covered her face with her hands. She could never face him again.

That's why he'd left her the car, and the message that he wouldn't be home tonight. He wanted to protect her from the shame and embarrassment of seeing him for as long as he could.

He really did care about her.

Just not the way she wanted him to.

* * *

Keenan went straight from *Sweet Bliss* to another strip club around the corner. He ordered a Jack Daniels and sat by the stage, staring at the naked women and hoping they'd drive the image of Lucy Barnaby out of his head.

It didn't work.

He'd never experienced a hunger like this. It clawed like a demon inside his chest.

Lucy . . .

It had taken all his strength to keep from coming in his pants—something he'd never done in a strip club no matter how intense the provocation.

But that lap dance . . . fuck, he was still hard just thinking about it. Maybe he should go to the men's room and jack off in a stall.

A few minutes later, he was back at the bar ordering another drink. He'd shot his wad all right, but it had barely taken the edge off.

He wanted Lucy. And now he knew he could have her.

So why the hell hadn't he driven her home, carried her into the empty house, and fucked her ten ways from Sunday?

Because it would be more than fucking with Lucy. It would mean something.

Keenan had never been a coward in his life. He'd conquered North Shore waves, the Iron Man triathlon, and every other challenge he'd ever faced. But he realized now that there was one thing he was afraid of.

He was afraid of getting his heart broken.

Until now, he'd never felt anything for a woman that went more than skin-deep. But he was in love with Lucy, and he'd never be able to take her body without giving her his heart.

Then she'd go back to the mainland. And when that happened, he'd be torn in two. He could follow her . . . but leaving Hawaii would break his heart as much as losing the woman he loved.

He was well and truly screwed.

An hour later, he left the club and flagged a taxi. He'd go to a friend's house tonight and start apartment-hunting tomorrow.

He opened his mouth to give his friend's address in Kapahulu.

Instead, he heard himself give his home address.

As the cab pulled away from the curb, he closed his eyes and leaned his head against the window. What the hell was he doing?

When they pulled up in front of his house, he realized exactly what he was doing.

He was going to Lucy.

He paid the driver and got out. Once the cab drove away, the street was dark and silent. Lucy was in the house, asleep.

He took a deep breath. The truth was, it was already too late to protect his heart. He already felt torn in two. And since his heart was going to break no matter what, why couldn't he have just one night with her?

He was pretty sure it would only be one night. She'd said that hearing him talk about sex had turned her on, but he knew from experience that imagining something and actually doing it were very different things. A lot of women fantasized about being dominated in bed, but found that they didn't enjoy the real thing.

Some of those women tried to go along with it anyway, figuring he wouldn't always be so alpha and that, over time, he'd "mellow out". But he knew himself well enough to know that he wasn't going to change. Eventually, the women he was with figured it out, too—and either ended things (if they didn't like it) or not (if they did). If not, then he usually broke it off himself after a few weeks, before things could get too deep.

But he was already in deep with Lucy.

One night. That's all he wanted. One night to bury himself in Lucy's sweetness, to take her the way he'd always wanted to. When she realized she preferred her fantasies about him to the real thing, that would be the end of it.

Maybe they could even go back to being friends.

It was a clear night, and the moon, almost full, was sinking towards the west. A gentle breeze blew, fragrant with plumeria.

He'd had a few shots of Jack that night, but it wasn't alcohol buzzing through his veins.

It was an excitement so intense he trembled.

He'd been fighting his attraction to Lucy for so damn long. Tonight he would finally give into it.

CHAPTER 7

Lucy usually slept on her side, and once she was out she slept pretty soundly.

Tonight she woke up only an hour after falling asleep, fuzzy-headed and confused. She was on her side, like usual, but her arms were—

In an instant she was as wide awake as if she'd been doused in icy water. Her wrists were bound behind her with something soft, like a stocking. She rolled onto her back and found herself looking into Keenan's black eyes.

He was kneeling on the bed beside her, and he was naked.

She realized suddenly that she was naked, too. She'd gone to bed in a camisole and panties, and both were gone.

A bolt of electricity went through her. She started to speak, but before she could say a word Keenan covered her mouth with his hand.

"I'm not going to gag you," he said softly, his eyes glittering in the moonlight. "And I'm not going to give you a safe word. If you say anything at all, I'll stop what I'm doing and untie you. But as long as you stay quiet, I'm going to do whatever I want. I'm going to take you hard, and I'm not going to ask if you like it. I'm going to make you come and I'm going to make you sore." He took his hand away. "Unless you tell me not to."

He looked down at her and waited.

Her heart was pounding hard enough to crack her ribs. Her mouth was dry. She wanted to say *yes, Keenan, please God yes*—but he'd made the rules very clear.

So she didn't say a word.

After a moment he smiled, but there wasn't anything sweet about it. It was a little bit wicked, and for the first time she felt nervous. What if she *didn't* like it? What if—

But before she could finish the thought, Keenan scooped her up in his arms, shifted on the bed so he sat with his back against the headboard, and settled her face down over his lap.

Her heart was beating wildly, her breath stuck somewhere in her throat. His erection pressed against the bare skin of her belly. The sensation sent a rush of heat between her legs, and all she wanted was to have that hardness inside her.

But when he rubbed his palm over her naked bottom, she knew Keenan had other plans for her first.

Oh, God. He was going to spank her.

Adrenaline made her heart rate spike. Would he tell her in a rasping, grating voice that she was a bad girl . . . that she'd teased him in the club that night and needed to be punished? Would he say—

But he didn't say anything. With no word and no warning he brought his hand down on her ass, and she had to bite her lip to keep from crying out.

It *hurt.*

The sting was like fire, and before she could recover he did it again, and again.

She managed to keep silent but she couldn't stop herself from writhing on his lap and trying to wriggle away.

Keenan laid a heavy hand on her bound wrists, holding her in place. She held her breath, waiting for his other hand to deliver another spanking, but it didn't come. Instead he trailed his fingertips gently over the skin of her bottom, soothing the burning sting. He stroked her softly, hypnotically, until she felt herself relaxing.

Then his hand slid lower, ghosting over the crack between her ass cheeks and settling over her pussy.

She went still.

At first he just kept his hand there, the warmth of his palm spreading slowly over her skin. Then, almost imperceptibly, his hand started to knead.

She bit her lip again, but this time it wasn't to keep from crying out.

It was to keep from moaning.

God, it felt so good.

Her whole existence seemed to center between her legs. Every nerve ending in her pussy seemed separately alive, quivering with pleasure. That big warm hand, covering her, massaging her . . .

And then something changed. Instead of his whole hand there was just one finger, tracing lightly over the very heart of her.

She was already wet, but now a rush of moisture came from her center as a pulse of excitement seared through her.

And still he only stroked her softly, lazily, as if he had all the time in the world. As if she weren't desperate for something more.

She couldn't speak, but she spread her legs a little wider, invitingly.

He didn't seem to notice. The rhythm of his touch didn't change. Just that one finger moving gently over her most sensitive skin, slick with her juices.

If he just stroked a little higher, he'd touch her clitoris. She *needed* him to touch her clitoris. She would die if he didn't touch her clitoris *right fucking now.*

She pressed her knees into the bed to raise her hips a little higher. She didn't care that she must look as shameless as a cat in heat. She was conscious only of desire, need, hunger.

But Keenan didn't give her what she wanted. He took his hand away completely, and she could have screamed in frustration.

Then he spanked her, hard, and the heat from the blow shot straight to her pussy.

Before she could recover Keenan lifted her off his lap and flipped her so she lay face up on the bed, her bound wrists behind her. He spread her legs roughly apart and moved between them, crouching over her like an animal.

She'd never felt so vulnerable. So exposed. A sudden flutter of fear went through her, and she almost told him to stop.

Then he fastened his mouth over her left breast.

She clamped her teeth on her bottom lip, willing herself to stay silent. She didn't want to do anything that would make him stop. His tongue was swirling around her nipple, teasing it to unbearable hardness as he used his fingers to tease and fondle her other breast.

His teeth grazed her skin, and the sensation made her arch her back to bring her closer to him.

Then his mouth was moving down her torso, his tongue dipping into her belly button before moving lower still.

Lucy had always been shy about oral sex. When the guys she'd been with had made their obligatory forays into the area, she'd told them she wasn't really into that.

None of them had seemed disappointed, which confirmed her suspicion that men didn't really enjoy going down on women.

Now it didn't even occur to her to say something, or to twist away. Instead she prayed that Keenan was heading where he seemed to be. For the first time in her life, she wanted to belong to a man that way. She wanted to be tasted.

Keenan closed his hands over her thighs and pushed them wider—as wide as they would go. Then he put his thumbs on her pussy lips and spread her wide there, too.

Oh, God.

Cool air made her shiver, and she realized he was blowing on her clitoris as his thumbs pressed harder and deeper into her soft flesh.

Then she felt his tongue.

She let out her breath in a long exhale as Keenan licked her slit from bottom to top and flicked his tongue against her clit, again and again until she started to shake.

Without warning, he slid three fingers inside her.

The sudden invasion made her moan, and for a second she froze, afraid she'd broken the rules. But Keenan began to thrust his fingers inside her, hard and rough and deep, even as the movements of his tongue intensified.

Her stomach muscles tightened. Her whole body tensed. And then she came, climaxing with such violence that she screamed.

Before she was even close to recovering Keenan pulled his fingers out of her and flipped her over on her stomach. She heard the sound of a foil packet tearing, and then he grabbed hold of her hips and jerked her to her knees.

With her hands bound behind her she couldn't support her weight with her arms. Her face was pressed into the bed. She turned her head to the side so she could breathe, and in the next instant Keenan's hands tightened on her hips as he slammed inside her.

She bit down on her pillow.

He was so. Fucking. *Big.*

His thrusts were ruthless. Savage. His hands gripped her like a vise, keeping her in place while he fucked her.

His right hand released her hip and he slapped her ass in time with his thrusts, over and over, harder and harder, until it felt like she was on fire. Then suddenly he moved that hand around to cover her clit, rubbing her there with brutal speed as his other hand slid up her back and into her hair.

One last thrust, and she felt his cock throb inside her as he came. The hand in her hair tightened, jerking her head up as he collapsed on top of her, and he sank his teeth into her neck as he shuddered out his release.

His body was heavy on hers but she never wanted him to move. She wanted to feel him on top of her forever, her pussy raw and sore and her clit throbbing in unbearable ecstasy. She wanted to feel the sting of his bite on her neck and the soft stroke of his tongue as he soothed the mark he'd left. She wanted to feel the wild pounding of his heart vibrating through her body. She wanted—

His weight lifted, and his hands were at her wrists. A moment later her arms were free.

Before she could miss the feeling of being bound and at his mercy, Keenan lay down beside her and pulled her back against him, wrapping his arms around her from behind and nuzzling her neck.

A feeling of peace soaked into her. Every muscle in her body was relaxed, every inch of her skin warm and tingling.

Would it be all right to talk now? She opened her mouth to say something—*that was incredible, oh my fuck-*

ing God, that was the best sex I ever had in my life—but the silence they were wrapped in seemed charmed, somehow, and she didn't want to break it. And what could she possibly say? The connection she felt with Keenan went deeper than language.

She closed her eyes and snuggled back into his arms.

They lay like that for a long time. Then, just as she was falling asleep, Keenan turned her gently so they were face to face.

Still they didn't speak. They looked into each other's eyes, and then Keenan pulled her to him for a kiss.

Our first kiss, she thought in a haze of pleasure. His mouth was soft, gentle . . . and his hands in her hair were gentle, too.

When the kiss finally ended he kept her close, holding her against his chest.

Lucy had never felt so safe, so wrapped in warmth and tenderness. She could hear the strong, steady beat of Keenan's heart.

This time she really did fall asleep.

* * *

In his whole life, Keenan had never felt like this.

He would never get enough of watching Lucy sleep. He, on the other hand, never wanted to sleep again.

He didn't want to miss a moment, a breath, a heartbeat.

Every so often a question about the future would surface in his mind, and he quelled it ruthlessly. He wouldn't think beyond tonight.

Tonight...

He couldn't believe she'd let him take her like that. Like he'd always fantasized. At the memory of it, his eyes closed and his cock hardened.

He wanted her again.

For a minute he tried to think of something else—something to distract him.

Then his eyes opened. This was his one night with Lucy, and he wasn't going to deny himself a goddam thing.

He leaned close, whispering in her ear as he covered her right breast with his palm.

"Wake up, Lucy."

She blinked and stretched like a cat, and his cock got even harder.

"What is it? Is something wrong?" she murmured.

"Nothing's wrong. I'm going to fuck you again."

Her eyes widened, and a spasm of fear went through him. Maybe she didn't want him anymore.

But then she whispered, "Oh God, yes. Please, Keenan—"

Her words made him drunk with pleasure.

A wave of tenderness overwhelmed him. Suddenly afraid that his heart was in his eyes, he forced himself to lie back, casually, with his arms folded behind his head.

"Put your mouth on me," he ordered her.

Her eyes widened again, and he heard himself add, "Unless you don't want to."

Jesus Christ. So much for the dominant male.

"I've wanted to go down on you for months," she said, and before he could say anything else she scooted down the bed and took him in her mouth.

He almost exploded right then and there. This was Lucy sucking him, Lucy's tongue moving up and down his cock, Lucy's hair shining like gold against his dark skin.

His breathing came harsher as he fought to keep from coming in her mouth. He'd dreamed about that, but his need to fuck her was even stronger.

"On your back," he growled when he couldn't take it anymore.

She looked up at him, her eyes dilated. "What?" she asked, her voice blurry with pleasure.

He put his hands on her upper arms and flipped them over, his weight pushing her into the mattress.

"On your back," he said again, his voice low and dark.

He kept his eyes on hers as he reached for one of the condoms he'd put on her bedside table, ripping it open with his teeth and sliding it on with one hand.

Then he pinned Lucy's wrists above her head and used a knee to part her thighs. She was panting as she looked up at him.

"Keenan..."

He drove into her hard, and she gasped.

He wanted to consume her. Devour her. He used his teeth on her throat and her breasts as he pounded into her, and her moans and cries almost drove him out of his mind.

Then her muscles clenched around him as her orgasm swept through her. The sensation drove him over the edge and he came, too, roaring her name and collapsing on top of her.

His heartbeat thundered against hers.

When he finally came back to earth he shifted onto his side and drew Lucy against him, her back to his chest. He wrapped his arms around her and pressed his lips into her hair.

This time when she fell asleep he did, too.

CHAPTER 8

Lucy woke slowly, blinking in the sunlight that spilled in through her window.

She smiled and stretched, remembering last night and hoping for a repeat this morning. Then she turned to face Keenan.

He wasn't there.

A moment of panic was followed by the stern application of logic. He was in the bathroom taking a shower, or in the kitchen making coffee. He'd be back in a few minutes.

A few minutes turned into half an hour. Finally, as logic gave way to fear, Lucy pulled on some clothes and went out into the hall.

Keenan's bedroom door was open. She looked inside and gasped.

Everything was gone. His bed was stripped; his drawers and closet were empty.

He'd moved out.

He'd fucking *moved out.*

She went into the living room and found Jessica curled up on the couch with a cup of coffee.

"Hey, Luce. How'd the lap dance go last night? I still can't believe you didn't tell me about this whole stripping thing."

Lucy sat down in the blue armchair. "It was fine," she said mechanically.

"Cool. So is this something you're going to be doing on a regular basis, or was it more of a one-time-only deal?"

"A one-time-only deal," she echoed.

That's what last night had been to Keenan. A one-time thing.

She'd fooled herself into believing they had some kind of connection, when the truth was, she didn't mean anything more to him than any of his other girls.

Her throat tightened and tears pricked her eyes. Then she lifted her chin, took a deep breath, and rose to her feet.

She was damned if she'd shed a single tear over the man who'd fucked her senseless, kissed her like Romeo kissed Juliet, and then snuck out of the house before sunrise.

"So . . . Keenan's gone, huh?"

Jessica nodded. "He packed up his stuff and left a couple hours ago. He wrote us a check for three months' rent, even though I told him it wouldn't take us that long to find a new housemate."

"Probably not." She cleared her throat. "I'm going to take a shower. Then I think I'll head to the university library to do some work on my thesis."

"Sounds good. Would you pick up some milk on your way back?"

"Sure."

As she stripped off her clothes in the bathroom and stepped into the shower, determined to wash every trace of Keenan from her skin, she decided to spend as much time pining over him as he'd spent with her after they'd made love.

And . . . done.

Time to move on.

* * *

When Keenan woke up that morning, the sun had just risen and a kind of panic gripped him.

He was in such a rush to pack his things and leave that he forgot his laptop in the living room. He came back for it a few hours later, parking around the corner and waiting in a neighbor's garage until he saw Lucy's car heading down the street.

She was gone.

His heart twisted in his chest as he headed towards the house. He knew it made him a coward, but he hadn't been able to face the whole morning-after thing with Lucy.

He was pretty sure she'd enjoyed herself last night—physically, anyway. But when he woke with her in his arms, still basking in the sweetest afterglow he'd ever experienced, fear had clawed at him.

What if, in the cold light of day, Lucy was disgusted by what they'd done together? He'd gotten that from women before. Hot and heavy at night; skeeved out in the morning. Sometimes they were mad at him, sometimes at themselves. Either way, any pleasure they'd felt disappeared in the face of accepting who he was in bed—his need to dominate, to be in charge.

That didn't happen much anymore . . . he'd gotten pretty good at sensing when a woman would click with him in bed. But none of his usual rules applied to Lucy. He'd wanted her so damn bad he would have risked anything to have her—including the look of revulsion in her eyes when morning came.

But when the gray light of dawn crept into the sky, he hadn't been able to face it.

And what if she didn't feel repulsed? What if she still wanted him? Wouldn't that be worse, in a way? Because if she still wanted him, he wouldn't be able to stay away.

He'd give himself to her, body and soul, and when she left it would rip his heart out.

It was better this way. A clean break.

Maybe if he said it to himself often enough, he'd start to believe it.

"Hey," Jessica said, looking up when he came through the door. "You just missed Lucy."

Her face and voice were normal, so Lucy hadn't filled her in on last night's activities.

"Where was she going?" he asked.

"The library, of course. Did you know you left your laptop here?"

"Yeah. That's why I came back."

The telephone rang as he passed it, and he picked it up automatically.

"Hello?"

"Is Lucy there?"

It was a man's voice, and his hand tightened on the phone. "No," he said. "Can I take a message?"

"This is her faculty advisor. Would you let her know I called?"

Keenan relaxed. He knew Adam Takamine; the professor was an old friend of his aunt's. He was also sixty years old and happily married.

"Hey, Adam, it's Keenan. I'll leave the message for Lucy."

"Hi, Keenan. I didn't recognize your voice. It's good news, so have her call me as soon as she can."

Good news?

It was none of his business, of course. But he heard himself ask, "What is it? Can you tell me?"

Adam chuckled. "It's pretty exciting. She was awarded the Shipton Fellowship for field research. If she accepts, she'll be funded for three years to study ancient hula. After that it'll be a cinch to get a spot with our faculty."

His brain seemed to be moving in slow motion.

"She . . . you mean . . . Lucy wants to teach *here*? In Hawaii?"

"Well, of course. Didn't she tell you? Maybe she was afraid to jinx it—the Shipton is competitive."

"She wants to teach here," he said again.

"That's right. And now it looks like she'll be able to."

He couldn't speak for a moment.

"Keenan? Are you there?"

"Yeah." He cleared his throat. "I'll have Lucy call as soon as she gets back. I know she'll be thrilled."

"Well, she deserves it. She's got the best brain in the department."

Yeah, she was smart . . . about everything but him.

He replaced the receiver and stared into space.

"What's up?" Jessica asked curiously. "Did Lucy get some good news?"

"Yeah."

"So what is it? And what the hell's wrong with you? You look sick to your stomach."

"I'm an idiot," he whispered.

"What?"

"I'm an idiot!"

Jessica stared at him. "Well, I won't argue the point."

He headed for the door.

"Hey! You're forgetting your laptop again."

He barely heard her. For the first time since he'd met Lucy Barnaby a year ago, he knew exactly what he needed to do.

* * *

Lucy couldn't concentrate worth a damn, but she kept on trying. Keenan had already fucked up her heart; she wasn't going to let him screw with her work, too.

She squeezed her eyes shut and opened them again, trying to focus on the article she was reading. Maybe if she took a coffee break she could—

The sound of a guitar broke into her consciousness.

She frowned as she looked up. The employees here were strict about the sacred silence of a library. It was hard to believe they'd let somebody—

Then she got her first glimpse of the musician.

It was Keenan.

He was dressed in Hawaiian formal wear—gray trousers and a white button-down shirt, with a beautiful

Maile lei around his neck. He was strumming his guitar in a melody she knew, singing a song that was more than a hundred years old.

> "Ua like no a like
> Me ka ua kani lehua
> Me he ala e i mai ana
> Aia i laila ke aloha
>
> O oe no ka u i upu ai
> Ku u lei hiki ahiahi
> O ke kani a na manu
> I na hola o ke aumoe.
>
> When the dews of the evening are falling
> Glistening on the flowers loved so well
> Then my heart to thee is calling
> From my place within the dell
>
> My heart, oh sweet, is there forever
> It thrills with love for thee alone
> Its constancy fades never
> I'll be ever true to thee, my own."

Everyone in the place, from students to librarians, had gathered around to listen. Keenan's voice and the beautiful sound of slack key guitar held everyone spellbound. When he finished, there was applause. And even though the senior librarian approached him immediately, there was a smile on her face.

Lucy stayed where she was. She hadn't clapped; she hadn't moved a muscle from the time she'd first seen Keenan. Now she watched him nod meekly as the librarian spoke, handing his guitar to her with a grin.

Then he looked at her.

An electric current seemed to pass between them. On her arms and the back of her neck, Lucy felt the fine hairs stand up. A kind of quivering tension rooted her to the spot as Keenan came towards her, his eyes never leaving hers.

A wave of heat whipped color into her cheeks as she remembered last night. The way she'd lifted her hips, begging him to touch her. The way he'd taken her, dominated her, overwhelmed her.

The way she'd responded, as though she'd been wanting him since . . .

Well, since the moment she first saw him.

Keenan stopped by her table and smiled down at her.

"Hey," he said softly. "Mrs. Palakiko suggested I take you outside if I have anything else to say." He held out a hand. "Will you come for a walk with me?"

She couldn't speak, so she just nodded. He helped her up and led her out into the quad.

They walked in silence for a few minutes, hand in hand. It was a beautiful day. Puffy white clouds chased each other across the cerulean sky and the sun was warm on their skin. The mountains that ringed Manoa Valley had never seemed greener; the air had never seemed sweeter.

When Keenan stopped she saw where he'd taken her.

"It's the Japanese garden," she said.

He nodded.

"This is my favorite place on campus."

"I know."

She looked at him. "You do?"

He turned to face her and took both her hands in his. "I know your favorite band is Cibo Matto. I know your favorite color is pink. I know your favorite flower is plumeria. I know your favorite perfume is Opium. I know your favorite writer is Jane Austen and your favorite book is *Emma*."

His hands tightened around hers. "I know that I've been in love with you for a year. I know that I kept coming up with reasons not to tell you—like the fact that you'd be going back to the mainland once you got your degree."

He paused. "Then, today, I took a phone message for you. You've won the Shipton Fellowship, Lucy."

She gasped. "I have? Really?"

He grinned. "Really. And when I heard you were interested in joining the faculty here, I realized something."

"What?"

"I realized that what I'm really afraid of is love. Because when I found out you might be staying in Hawaii, I wasn't relieved. I was scared shitless. Because I didn't have another reason not to be with you . . . except for one." He took a breath. "I've always been afraid that if you knew what I was like in bed, you wouldn't want anything to do with me."

"But you told me what you were like in bed the first month I knew you. And all those stories you told . . . it's not like you hid it."

"Yeah, I know. That's the other way I kept myself from making a move on you. Every time I saw the look in your eyes when I talked about sex, it was a reminder that we didn't belong together."

She raised one eyebrow. "The look in my eyes was lust."

He laughed a little shakily. "I didn't know that. And even when you told me . . . let's just say I wasn't convinced. I've known women who thought they wanted what I was offering, but figured out that the real thing is a little different. And I've never been willing to change who I am in the bedroom."

His hands tightened again. "Until now. If you'll be with me, Lucy, I can change."

"You mean . . . change sexually?"

"Yeah."

Warmth spiraled out from her heart and through her whole body. "Well, that's very nice of you. But there's one problem."

His face tensed. "What?"

"I don't want you to change. I fucking *love* how you are in the bedroom. Are you telling me you didn't notice that last night? Were my two orgasms not enough?"

He stared at her. "I . . ."

"Last night was the best sex I've ever had in my life. Partly because I loved what we did, and partly because—" She paused, and took her courage in both hands. "Because I love *you*. I've been in love with you forever, Keenan."

For a minute neither of them said a word. They stood in the Japanese garden and stared into each other's eyes, letting emotion course between them.

After a while they started walking again, wandering through the garden in a glow of joy.

"Why did you come into the library all dressed up?" she asked finally. "And singing that song?"

"That's how my father proposed to my mother."

When he saw the expression on her face he laughed out loud. "Don't worry—I'm not proposing. Not yet, anyway," he added with a grin. "But after being such a dick for so long, I thought you deserved an apology. A big one. And since you danced for me, I thought the least I could do was sing for you."

Her heart welled up until it threatened to overflow. "Since you're not proposing, what exactly *are* you asking me?"

He raised her hand to his mouth and kissed it. "Will you be my girlfriend, Lucy?"

They stopped under the coral shower tree near the tea house.

"Yes," she whispered.

He framed her face with his hands. "I love you."

"I love you, too."

He bent his head to kiss her. And as she rose up on her toes and slid her arms around his neck, it occurred to Lucy that home isn't always a place.

Sometimes it's a person.

ABOUT THE AUTHOR

Kate Grey believes that a good love story should make you sigh and a good love scene should make you squirm—in the best possible way. Her dream is to find the perfect balance between romantic and sexy, and since she's fairly certain she'll never reach that goal, she's probably going to be writing for a long, long time. She's currently at work on her fourth book.

She loves to hear from readers and can be reached at kategreywrites@gmail.com.

Books by Kate Grey

By His Desire
His One Desire
Only Desire

Printed in Great Britain
by Amazon